T0157934

Indelicate Things

Indelicate Things

A Collection of Narratives About the
Female Body Giving and Receiving Pleasure.

RUTH MARIMO

authorHOUSE®

AuthorHouse™
1663 Liberty Drive
Bloomington, IN 47403
www.authorhouse.com
Phone: 1 (800) 839-8640

Published by AuthorHouse 05/28/2015

ISBN: 978-1-5049-0635-7 (sc)
ISBN: 978-1-5049-0636-4 (hc)
ISBN: 978-1-5049-0634-0 (e)

Library of Congress Control Number: 2015905835

Print information available on the last page.

"Indelicate Things ~ These Pronouncements we both make, even our words blush"

- Heather Sticka

Contents

You Caught My Eye

The music is loud, the club is crowded, I buy a drink and look around for someone I know or some place where I can move, but there's no space and all the faces are a blur that's when I first see you, our eyes meet for just one short moment, I turn away but I feel yours still on me, following me wherever I go. Every time I turn I feel you looking, calmly circling, mentally peeling me away, layer by layer, through my clothes, past my naked body, into my skin until you meet my soul, my last inner place, no secret of mine is safe, you know what I'm thinking, every time I turn you are there. I can feel you watching, it takes my breath. I shiver, I'm scared of how it makes me feel, yet I am exhilarated, I know this is what I want, yet I want to run. I close my eyes and wrap an arm around myself imagining that it's yours I feel your breath, your presence, I ache for your touch, I know that it is safe, will protect me that your arms will defend me. I turn around and you are still there, calmly looking, the noise the crush of the people are invisible, my heart pounds, my mouth goes dry, I know I can't escape yet I know I must run my whole body comes alive for one moment. Maybe I am imagining this, wishing it, desiring it but I know that it is real. I try to push the thoughts out of my head, my mind is crowded, confused, the room is hot; the music is so loud, exotic, rhythmic. I try to walk the dance floor to the bathroom, bodies are pushed together, and I squeeze between them there's barely any room to get through. I look up it's you, I turn but you block my way with your body, I gulp and look around for a way to escape, but my body doesn't want me to, I feel my heart race, the adrenalin soar. My entire body shudders. I smile & say excuse me, I smile and laugh but unconvincingly, but you don't smile back; you're staring deep in my eyes. I act annoyed I turn again, but I know what you've come for, in my mind I'm screaming for you to fuck me; you won't let me move, the crowd surges and presses us together, I feel the heat of your body, your physical presence. The crowd loosens, I break free. I get to the bathroom I'm out of breath and I splash water on my face and hold a towel to my face when I open my eyes I see you standing by the door in the reflection of the mirror, blocking my escape, Deep down I've been craving for so long for the touch of another woman, I never knew how bad I wanted a beautiful femme butch. I let a little cry out, I want it so bad but as much as I ache I am so afraid, I clean myself up in the sink. I notice a wet spot on my top. I think to myself I've been aching for so long to be taken now that this is it I wonder if I'm just imagining the whole thing. I know I'm not, I turn around and we are both standing there alone staring at each other.

2

My Dream

As soon as I got home and laid my head on my pillow, closing my eyes you met me there.. Naked you stood before me, your tanned skin flawless, your hair with a shade matching your complexion, your eyes staring, your smile wide and radiant.. The first thing I want to do is pull you in bed and have my way with you, but you're not having it, this time you want to be in control. You start by undressing me, pulling my shirt above my head, undoing my bra, you move down to my pants and unbutton them, then you yank them off of me, surprisingly you leave my panties on. You lay on top of me, holding my hands down to my sides with each of yours, our nipples touching. You start to kiss me, our tongues do a dance, your kisses are so wet and your saliva keeps dripping into my mouth, I swallow as much as I can, you begin to suck on my tongue so hard that it feels like you will pull it right out of my throat.. I gasp in pleasurable pain, you seemed timid and shy, inexperienced but you're showing me a different side of you, you're so

3

eager to please me today. You move your mouth to my neck and ears, my chin then my nipples, with a flick of your tongue you start on one, then the other and you go back and forth and the sensation you're giving me is driving me wild. I start to push your head down gently, anxious to feel your tongue and mouth around my engorged clitoris but when you remove my panties and come face to face with it, you hesitate. You have never licked another girls' pussy before and you are unsure.. I start to plead with you, begging you 'please baby please' I need you to, want you to. I raise my hips so my smooth and shaven pussy sits right at your chin & like magic I watch and see you whip your tongue out and lick tasting me for the first time, I can feel the trickle of wetness going down my ass. You just get me so excited, you lick the clear liquid right from my center and without hesitating I see you swallow it. You get comfortable and suck my entire lips into your mouth, then let go and lick up and down and in circles. I have waited so long for you to please me this way that I can't contain my orgasm any longer, I hold your head firmly down as I contract and shiver and shake.. You don't stop, you lick me until I calm down cleaning me up with your tongue..

I hump the bed in my sleep, wake up and realize it was all just a dream..

Pure Yearning

Don't think for a second I've forgotten how it feels to have your gaze on

me... That deep gaze that shoots at me from your big and bright green

eyes anytime I'm in the same room as you... It doesn't matter who else is

around, I remember a time when the man you loved stood right next to

you but you couldn't stop yourself from being transfixed at every curve

on my body and when I embraced you with a friendly goodbye hug you

ran your hands up and down my torso, pulling me in but unable to keep

holding on to me... On the drive home I kept thinking about how wet

you could be... But alas you had a man and you could not yet tell me the

ways in which I moved you... & yet again everything we are and are

not became too blurred and too conflicting so you did what you always

do... You ran... I let you be... But here we are again... I don't know how

it is we find ourselves in this dark room... I don't know if you recognize

that my scent has changed from the last time you placed wet kisses and

gentle bites across my neck... But your intoxicating mouth is still the same, every graze of your teeth against my flesh sends chills down my spine and all across the rest of my body... As if every fiber of my being is encoded with the memory of your lips... Your skin against my hands feels much softer than I remember and I take my time reminding you of how my hands felt against you... I move from cupping each of your breasts to gently stroking the sides of your body, the curves of your hips, the roundness of your buttocks... My mouth finding yours and all at once we are lost in that time and space the world ceases to exist... You forget how much you can't stand me at times and I forget how long you've stayed in denial.. In this moment all is forgiven... I am wet and hungry for you... You're pulling me close, digging your fingernails into my back as if you want our bodies to magically merge into one... I anticipate the feel of your silky wetness against my fingertips, the swelling of your clitoris in my mouth, the tight ridges and heat that greets my fingers when I enter you... I just want to fuck you so bad but that thing you do, when you bite my bottom lip and keep me there, makes me pause and as soon as you free me, my lips move down your neck as I push you gently against the wall, taking your top off as soon as the wall secures you... The bra must go too... My hands and mouth kneading your breasts so gently... Gently biting your nipples at intervals until I hear you gasp.. Your fingers in my hair... Subconsciously pushing me down but I keep my mouth at your breasts while my hands gently caress your hips... I can feel the heat radiating from in between your legs... I want to feel this heat against my face... I move down your body planting rushed wet kisses on your belly until I'm kneeling before you, my lips touching your clit as you part your legs and give me access to the most sacred part of

you.. You're dripping wet... I taste you with one long stroke followed

by another ever so slowly and gently that all you can do is whimper

and guide my head with your hands... By the time my fingers find

themselves wrapped inside your warm ridges... You're flooding me with

your orgasm... But the night is still young...

Tonight I Want to Make Love You

Of course there is absolutely nothing wrong with the way we fuck, I love to fuck you and love to have you fuck me but baby tonight I want to make love to you. Before you get home from work I'm rushing, I have rose petals sprinkled from the door to our bed and then another trail to our master bath where a bubble filled bath awaits us. I have your favorite ice bucket filled with ice and your favorite champagne bottle chilling inside it... I had to scribble 'I love you' on the note I have sitting next to the two dozen peach colored roses I have arranged for you in a crystal vase on our cherry oak table. The only scent that fills our chateau is that of burning candles, in this space that's only ours. No they won't be a meal tonight my darling for my plan is to feast on you, to quench my thirst with your sweet nectar and fill all my senses with everything that is you. At last I hear that little knock of yours as you shuffle with your keys at the door.. My heart starts to flatter, am I forgetting anything? Is everything perfect? You walk in and I greet you with a tall glass of champagne, I seal the offer with a kiss.. Your eyes are wide scanning the room you want to say something but my lips are still locked on yours... This power you have over me, overwhelms me, renders me weak, I could rip your clothes off right now right here like I usually do but baby tonight I want to make love to you. I resist the temptation, take your hand and follow the rose petals on the carpet, first to our bedroom where I help you out of your leather coat and shoes and then to our bathroom, I undress you slowly not saying much, taking you all in once again. The lingering smell of your Viva LA Juice Couture perfume, Ohhh the shimmer of your bronze skin, the lemon roundness of your breasts, the goose bump like little cute bumps around your nipples, the flatness of your belly, the soft curves of your hips. You step in the tub and I undress and follow, I start by lathering every inch of you with a soapy fluffy sponge, only stopping to take sips of the bubbly champagne, you're rubbing me too, I can see the fire in your eyes.. You towel me I towel you, my mouth is on you now, giving you soft kisses starting with that area between your neck and the beginning of your chest. I need to lay you down, I take you to the bed, you're face down on our plush bed and I'm laying on you, can you feel the softness of my breasts on your bare back? I'm giving you soft wet kisses all down your spine, massaging you at the same time, being careful not to miss any piece of flesh, I make my way down to your round ass both hands massaging, my teeth lightly biting this muscle of your body, I run my tongue all the way up the crack of your ass, my hands help me part these bountiful mountains. Letting the saliva build on my tongue before licking right on your asshole, around and in, you taste so clean, so amazing.. I can hear you whimper you're desperately clinging on to the cover of the bed, as if you want to escape this torturous pleasure I'm giving you but I'm holding you back, holding you tight, you're safe in my arms. I move to your thighs licking the length of them, the inner part of your knees are so sensitive when I kiss and lick you there, your moans are mixed with your adorable giggles.. You don't notice me slip an ice chip from the bucket into my mouth before I turn you over.. And right away I'm straddling you.. But I move to face your perfect tits.. Before I touch them with my lips I let ice cold droplets of water fall across each nipple from my mouth, you freeze in place, shocked by the coldness of it all, but don't worry I'll warm you as I let my tongue warm up with the suckling of each nipple, the long strokes around and underneath each breast... You know it's one of my favorite parts on you, it sets you apart from the rest, for no one has such perfect breasts as yours... You have my pussy dripping wet now, I leave traces of my wetness across your thighs and belly as I move to scissors you with my legs... I want to feel the wet and warm silkiness of your pussy against mine, I want to rub my clit against your clit, as I anchor myself down on you can you feel how wet and excited I am for you? Do you feel the colorless nectar of my lust for you as it blends with yours? In that part that's most private on your body... At last we touch, connect and yes the sky does part, the fireworks do explode.. Our sounds drown any other sound my Aaahhhhhhhsss, your OooooHhhhs. We are grinding against each other so fiercely and yet so slowly while we kiss deeply and passionately, the wet and sloppy kisses you know I love, the kind of kisses that force you to drink me, drink from my mouth, taste and swallow me... We have a steady and rhythmic pace going, there is now a thin film of sweat covering each of our bodies.. I can feel you getting there by the sudden sharp hike of your moans by the tightening of your grip on me, you're digging your nails into my back, I'm sucking the blood out of your neck like a hungry vampire... Ohhh Cum for me baby.. Cum for me,,, I'm Cumming, I...'m Cummmmmming you barely respond... You're so fucken sexy and this is driving me wild... My head bursts and my river raptures, can you feel the hot liquid I'm squirting on you, soaking, drenching your amazing slit... You Cum too right at that moment, wave after wave washes over you... I'm dizzy and blinded by passion and even though your pussy is a complete mess of our love making.. I lower my mouth down.. I can't make love to you without licking the very thing I long to quench my thirst.....

While You Cook

Now that I've made you mine, I can picture you in the kitchen, standing by the stove cooking, unaware that I'm watching you from the door, admiring the view of your backside, your smooth and long legs make me move closer to you.. I scare you a bit as I stand behind you, my hands massaging your chest through your t-shirt, my mouth nibbling at your neck, you lean your body all the way against mine, you're moaning already, your breathing getting heavier as I move my hands up and down your belly, I put one hand underneath your t-shirt and I love the softness of your skin, my other hand is moving further down your waist, trying to gain entry into your shorts and panties.. I find the treasure I'm looking for, I stroke you up and down with my wet fingers.. I have you so wet already.. Hadn't planned on making love to you right here, but you're begging me.. To enter you 'Please baby please' I hear you say but a woman as fine as you should never have to ask.. I turn you around and lift your t-shirt up just to reveal your gorgeous breasts, I lift the bra off of them as I kiss you passionately on the lips. You are a good kisser and you taste delicious I move my mouth down your neck, and then your nipples while my hand is working in-between your legs, I find your g-spot with two fingers.. You push against my hand with both your hands wanting me to remain right where I am, wanting me to go deeper, you spread your legs further, I start to add and subtract fingers in and out of you as you move up and down against my hand. I continue to lick and bite with my mouth, you're shaking now, I can feel your muscles contracting against my fingers deep inside of you.. I have you almost in tears now.. You start screaming 'I love you.. I love you' as you climax completely drenching my fingers and your juices dripping down my hand.. I hold you tight and whisper in your ear.. 'I love you too'…

When You're Mad

You getting mad at me or upset and wanting I guess to let go of me totally had me thinking of what that would be like if I could actually see you. I can tell you're quiet but I bet when something pisses you off, you really get mad. I think it would be hot, I can picture you pushing me away from you as I try to apologize and pull you towards me. You are telling me not to touch you or come near you but the more you tell me the more I want to just rip your clothes off. I keep coming towards you until I have you pinned against the wall, you still want to fight but my lips are on you now shutting you up. You can no longer resist me and you kiss me back tears streaming down your face because it upsets you this seeming power I have over you but you can't help it. You make me want you in the worst way when you get mad and throw a fit, I start to move down with my mouth as you stand against the wall. All I want to do is taste you, I kneel before you and kiss around your inner thighs, I can see your panties are wet, I remove them slowly and my tongue takes their place, licking, sucking. You're trying to grab the wall, pull my hair, hold my shoulders.. You just don't know what to do with yourself. You start to moan and cry all at the same time, you can no longer deny that no one else has ever made you feel this way, ever made you climax with just the warmth, wetness and skill of their tongue and mouth against the most private part of you..

I guess that's my way of saying I'm sorry.

That Picture of You

All I have to do is take a look at that picture of you for me to be once again reminded of the time when I first noticed the true beauty of a woman, a surging of flashback images of first my history teacher ever so slender, such caramel skin, could she tell when I always made excuses to be near, when I had never ending questions in her class just so she could take one more look at me, pay attention to me just one more time. Then a year or two later that crush fades but then a new one begins this time she is my Geography teacher, and yes just from that picture of yours I can see clearly now that it was more than her pretty face or the dark tone of her brown skin, that what really drew me to her was the shape of her breasts, how they sat at attention on her chest beckoning me to look their way, stealing my concentration as I tried to listen to the lessons she taught. That picture of you, yes the one in which you bare your chest, the one you trusted only for my eyes to see, takes me back, back to the days of changing rooms after basketball tournaments and girls of all shapes, brown shades and sizes walking freely about these rooms, naked, some in showers, some sitting on the wooden lockers completely unaware of how they took my breath away.

It is that picture of you that suddenly reminds me that even though finally I gave in and had a taste of womanness, I'm still to taste one with whom I bare the same roots, one who understands my foreign tongue, one who totally gets me, one who recognizes this passion I have inside that burns like the markings of a hot iron tattoo, this passion that keeps me awake at night, this dream that takes me places ordinary minds won't dare go. That picture of you that makes me wish your womb could carry my third child, for I know they would be no arguments on what our little beautiful person would be called, my choice Chiedza, our ray of sunshine and if your choice was Rumbidzai or even something more unique like Ruvarashe I would protest not for you're so deserving of my understanding. It is that picture of you that tells me that even if that was so and this fantasy I've created were to come true it would be grueling, the families who will never be supportive or understanding, the culture that's very much ours that would be so quick to shun us, the despair of not ever being able to partake in a traditional wedding ceremony with the ambuyas and sekurus dancing and ululating hysterically, so happy that at last we have found each other and will work to make a family, no, we would never see pride written on our mothers faces but then again it is that picture of you that shows me the power a woman like you possesses, shows me that if wishes were horses and beggars could ride then the distance wouldn't exist between us, that with instantaneous apprehension somehow we could be, wouldn't that just be perfect? You with your big dreams of being a world famous model, poet and so much more, mine of being an author like none other, a provider and still pursue my PHD in nursing because of course one day I would have to write books to teach doctors and nurses truly how to care for their patients.

It is in that picture of yours where I can see just what a terrible combination of fuels a relationship between us would be, for in all my life I'm yet to meet anyone with as similar a personality to mine as you. Of course the love making and fucking would be the best either of us has ever had, me trying to please you more than all the women before me have, you trying to show me everything no other woman has, the happy times would be amazing and the love filled with notes and pieces worthy of a Nobel prize, but the fights would just be as bad, the screams during arguments, I know I can control myself, but could you resist the urge to slap me across the face when you have failed to get your point across any other way? Would you be jealous if I got famous enough to have a million adoring fans? Would you believe that I loved only you when women throw themselves at me? Would I be happy knowing every man that sees you wants to fuck you like I do, would I be jealous of your ex the one who will always have a piece of your heart. Would I ever be able to break an innocent woman's heart all for this fantasy.

That picture of you tells me that we will have many secrets to keep, tells me that we will always be intrigued by the other's life somehow, that we will have feelings of yearning and yet deny them or downplay them.... that picture of you spells we have the same first initial and that we're but dreamers and dreamers we are.

Your Cunt

It isn't that your gorgeous face or your exquisite mouth didn't welcome me,

they did, with that olive skin interrupted by beautiful brown dots every few inches and those delicate sweet kisses on my lips and my other lips.

But baby your cunt, she blew me away.

How can she be so vast, have birthed two children and entertained other lovers before me and yet she molds perfectly into me?

She yields to my commands, even when I know she has so much strength and so much courage.

Allows herself to be vulnerable with me, whispers gently to the places on my body I cannot even name.

Is a brilliant beam of light that shines before me as if every-time I'm near her it is a near drowning experience.

She makes me feel chosen, special, she thinks my skin is the perfect shade and the perfect shape, she adores my fingers to the bone, she coats my lips with honey.

Everyday she puts on a different scent for me, as if to keep me from being content, a sweet surprise as unpredictable as Nebraska weather.

Sometimes all I want to do is beg, but she isn't easily moved.

She isn't afraid or apologetic, she doesn't pretend to be full when she is hungry.

She wears her hair however she wants like a feminist, she has more layers than I could count..

Even if I had eternity, I would still be discovering all she is.

Please allow my adulation, always keep me hidden within her walls...

in that space your breath is weighted and my eyes are glossy and my conscience slipping.

When we have both crossed over to another realm of life where only you and I exist.

Don't Forget to Wear Your Dick

With this lovely but daunting task we have of always having to run after

our kids and my night shift schedule we barely ever have private time

to ourselves, especially during the week so we have made our special

time the forty five minutes or so we lock ourselves in our bathroom to

take a shower and no matter how much our kids knock, whine and gripe

at the door we just have to ignore their calls.. For this is our time of the

day. It's 9pm & in two hours I have to be at work, I go in the shower first

while you finish up settling the kids but you soon join me, you come

in holding the velvet bag of ours and I already know what's on your

mind, I continue to brush my teeth with my set of our matching spin

toothbrushes with an obvious smile now across my face, you're trying

to hide your grin, I set the shower water temperature just how we like

it, Hot and Steamy... I step in and close the shower curtain behind me

teasing you, you frantically brush your teeth, thank God the toothbrush

is electric because in five seconds flat you're done brushing your teeth and under the steaming faucet with me, you soak your hair while I stare at the marvelous work of steel that is your body, I lather myself up, grab my razor and touch up my armpits and my pussy making sure I leave them as smooth and hair free as you like it, don't worry my legs are stubble free as well. We take turns rinsing off under the shower, now and then planting kisses on each other's lips and and water soaked cheeks, I step out first and dry myself off because lucky for me I didn't have to get my hair wet. I lotion myself and it takes you longer to dry off, you finally wrap the big towel around your head to help you dry your hair and as you reach for the lotion bottle you look at me and say 'Don't forget to wear your Dick', as you look at the bag sitting on the floor, I pick the bag up and shuffle through the various vibrators and dildos we have until I pull out the 8" strap-on that you like me to fuck you with. I tightly fasten it around my thin frame as I look at my reflection in the mirror.. With my C-cup size tits that look fake as I'm so skinny and now my 8" sized dick, I look like those paintings of half man half beast... I move towards you, turn you around so you're facing me as I sit you on the granite counter of our bathroom, our mouths and lips are engaged in a wrestling battle, when I get a hold of your tongue I suck on it as hard and long as I can until yours overpowers me and does the same to mine, your legs are wide open and my body sits between them, your hands are all over my huge breasts, yours are smaller than mine just the way I like it, I'm squeezing yours with both my hands never breaking the kiss, I run my tongue across your top then your bottom teeth, then I lick the corners of your mouth before I start to lightly bite at your chin, you love when I do this, then soon I'm breathing hot air against your right ear before slowly tracing its insides with my warm tongue, this really drives you wild, I bet you're wet and I want to find out; so with my right hand I move in-between your thighs and with my middle finger I start from the soft but dry top of your clitoris until I reach the silky moist center of your vagina, I continue to play with you this way, my tongue in your ear, my finger stroking you, my left hand on your tits and your hands and mouth all over me.. I'm so hot now all I want to do is fuck you, without me saying a word you go on all fours on the bathroom floor, my favorite way to fuck you, I kneel behind you and my 8" borrowed penis lines with your ass, I grab a hold of it as I guide it into your sweltering cunt, I begin a slow fuck just so you can get used to it once again since we haven't used it in a while, but in a few minutes it's you who begins to reverse fuck me by pulling away from me then slamming your ass back into me hard, taking the whole 8" in. I guess you're ready to be fucked, ready to be my bitch, my slut and no baby not at all in a bad way. I lean forward against your body so my tits are against your back and my left hand is touching the floor for support while I move my right hand underneath of you to stroke your clitoris from side to side with all my fingers while pumping you much HARDER now, much DEEPER.. You start to cry out, you're in ecstasy.. I could CUM right now because shit fucking you like this is unbelievable, I almost forget that the dick is plastic and not really mine because each time I push this thing deep within your magical walls, I feel an electric current through my pussy that quickly spreads to the rest of my body... Oh Fuck baby, Shit, this is sooo good... I can feel the

23

burning of my knees as they start to bruise from the constant rubbing against the tiled floor.. I'm not sure how long I can hold on but lucky for me, your hands and knees are starting to tire as well, you push me out of you, and you're so annoyed that you have to have me stop FUCKING you even for just one second, you're on your back now and you eagerly pull me back, I enter you missionary style and for the first time our bodies are in complete contact with each other, breasts to breasts, arms to arms.. You spread your legs even wider as you grab my ass cheeks with both your hands.. Helping me Fuck you harder, deeper, I go behind your neck with my hands and grab on to your hair and with each pump I enforce on you, I lightly tug at your hair, literally riding the shit out of you... We're sweating profusely, I can see the sweat from my neck drip down to your chest.. We're both moaning so loud, you're screaming my name and tears start to fall from your eyes, I love it when I fuck you to complete tears, dominate you in such a way that you completely surrender yourself to me.. Make me your Goddess you already know you're mine. I can't hold back any longer you've brought me to tears by your utter submission.. I feel as if I may just lose consciousness as I reach the peak of my climax, when you hear this you can't help your orgasm either, we're CUM FUCKING now.. We just can't stop, we're exhausted, why lord, why does fucking you have to be so damn magical.. I finally slide out of you and with the little energy I have left I unfasten the strap and toss the drenched thing in the sink.. Its use is done for the day but you're far from being done with me.. We have completely lost track of time, oh well I can be late for work for once.. I rinse my hands and get back to you on the floor, you're laying face down, I slide my thumb into you and hook it, locating your g-spot and I stroke you there, back and forth... When your moans increase in sound I move my body on top of you, while continuing with my thumb motion, I lay on you with my crotch against your fine ass and I start to hump you as I massage your g-sport, you move both your hands underneath of yourself so you can stimulate your clit, we're both pleasuring you now.. Your breathing deepens as if your very soul is trying to escape you, 'OHhh OHh, I LOVE You, I LOVE YOU', you moan in a voice I don't even recognize.. This makes me cum instantly.. My cum slides down your ass crack all the way to my thumb that's steady fucking you still.. You're cumming for me, tell me you're cumming for me.. You know how much I love to hear it, tell me you're all mine.. 'I'm cummming baby' you cry, 'I'm cumming my sweet sweet lover, I'm yours, I'm yours', 'Take me I'm yours' you say as we lay like that, with nothing but the loud beating of our hearts and the short breaths we're trying to catch... I don't get to fuck you often but boy when I do it's heavenly, I think to myself.

New Girl in Town, She Gives Me the Green Light

It's a warm and vibrant evening, I'm sitting outside Blue Sushi restaurant down town having cocktails with my girlfriend, I'm being silly trying to cheer her up because of course once again I've made her upset by complaining about how long it takes her to get dressed and how tired I was of us always showing up late to anything we're invited to. I must say the Margaritas in this place are extra strong tonight, I've already had my favorite cocktail 'under the sun', I swear with one sip of that drink I'm sitting on a beach in Belize' somewhere... Just then a friend walking on the busy sidewalk notices us and comes over, leaning into the rail she wakes me from my day dream with her "what's up girls?",

"Heyyy",

me and my girl respond in unison, "what are you up to?'"

I ask..

"Ohhh nothing just hanging down town with some friends, you know".

She is about to walk off but then she remembers something, and that's when she calls you over from the group of girls that are waiting for her, as you approach us that's when I first notice you, you look absolutely stunning in your little black dress and heels, your hair looks amazing, you're clutching a small black purse in one hand.... "Oh this is Ropa, my friend"

she says,

"she is Zimbabwean, just moved here last week, I'm showing her around"

Before I can say anything my friend looks to you and says, "now this is the person you want to meet",

pointing at me, "she knows how to have a good time"

If my complexion wasn't so dark you would have all seen my cheeks turn a rosy red with my blushing at this statement and the piercing look you're giving me now, I act unmoved and extend a hand out to you in greeting, "Zimbabwean huh", I think to myself but out loud I say,"

such a pleasure to meet you"

My friend is saying you have to get going and I have to think quickly...

"Hey you have a number yet?"

I find the courage to say,

"you know so we can all do something together sometime",

obviously trying not to make my white girlfriend feel left out.. "Yes"

you reply and start yelling out your number while I put it in my phone..

"Ropa, right? is that how you say it?",

"well it's short for Ropafadzai",

you giggle,

"and I have to run, nice to meet you".

You take off and my girl looks at me and says, "oh she is cute",

I say, "I don't see it",

just in case she is testing me, just to start another fight... The rest of the evening is uneventful, except for just a lingering thought of our brief introduction as I close my eyes to sleep. Having made an excuse of being too tired for sex.

The very following Saturday my girlfriend has some family thing to attend out of town and I have been invited to a very elaborate party in a fancy part of town. I certainly wasn't showing up by myself, that's when I think of calling you, maybe just to be friendly and polite, just to see if maybe you were not busy and we could just hang out, maybe just maybe you would give me the green light, you know maybe just give me one night.... I'm nervous as I click your name on my contact list, the phone is ringing now... "Hello",

"Hey, ahh Hi, ya it's me you know we met last Saturday downtown",

"Oh ya, this is a pleasant surprise, how are you?",

"Oh good, well bored right now, wondering if you want to do something tonight, I have a party to go to and no one to go with"

I pause, my heart pounding because I'm sure it's late notice and being the new girl in town, someone else must have already included you in their plans.. But lucky for me you say,

"sure, can you pick me up?",

"of course", I respond.

I get the details to your apartment and I've lived in this town so long I don't need directions to get anywhere. Around 8pm I'm standing outside your door, I pause before I knock.. Look myself over one more time, I always try to have just enough masculinity to balance my femininity.. I have a lacy black shirt on, low cut jeans, big belt, black opened toed heels, I like to wear my hair long, keeps me feminine, I love to smell good, so I can sense the presence of my Euphoria Perfume by Calvin Klein as I stand here in front of your door, anxiously awaiting to see what lies on the other side of it, I can hear your foot steps as you approach the door and can immediately tell you have heels on but when you open the door, my jaw almost falls to the floor, you look gorgeous, you have on a short short black tight fitting leather skirt, the heels are knee high leather heels and you have a sleeveless tee with a vest on top. Why would you do this to me, my plans were completely innocent right up to the point I saw you dressed this way, I had introduced my girlfriend to you the other night, but I'm not sure if you understood that she was my girlfriend as in I am a lesbian. I say you look great, you say I do too and we head out to my car, on the drive there you're not very talkative, it must be your personality. I want to say a lot but I don't want to scare you with my craziness. We get there and the place is packed, people are dressed to kill and drinks are flowing. There are little bars set up in every corner of this place and to break the ice I offer you a cocktail, you prefer Martinis... I introduce you as the new Zimbabwean in town to all my friends, "I'm just showing her around",

I emphasize because clearly everyone knows I have a girlfriend. You seem to be having a good time blending in, you give me glances every once in a while, we dance to the hot and loud music, keeping a little distance, just dancing like girls do, we're both getting a little tipsy, you start to open up a bit, start asking me questions about where in Zimbabwe I grew up and the schools I attended. The evening keeps getting better, we have to lean into one another's ears as we talk because of the noise in this place.. You're drinking these drinks like a fish in water and so am I. I excuse myself to find a bathroom, I'm told to go up

stairs to a secluded part of the house, when I get there I cool off and try
to freshen up, I start looking through the bathroom cupboards and to my
surprise I see a basket full of sex toys one of which is a vibrating black
strap on.. I'm instantly horny just by looking at this find, I never meant
for things to turn out this way but now I know that tonight whatever
it takes I have to fuck you, in this very bathroom, I'm going to show
you just what your body has been missing. When I return to you, I'm
annoyed as I see you dancing with some guy.. Being that I'm tipsy now,
I become possessive as I butt in, the dude raises his hands like what the
fuck is up and you have the same look on your face..,

"what's wrong with you?"

You ask,

"Oh I'm gone for one minute and some dude is already up your ass",

is my drunken response.

"WHAT??? You're not my date, why would you say something like that".

I immediately realize that I have crossed the line and I start to apologize,

"gees I'm sorry, I lost it for one second, can you forgive me".

You storm off,

"where is the bathroom you ask?"

As you walk away, I chase after you,

"it's up stairs",

I say, running ahead of you, when I get to the bathroom door I open it and I usher you to enter, and instead of closing the door and standing outside I walk in too, and lock the door behind us. You sit and start to urinate on the toilet your hands clasping your face as you try to ignore me. I'm standing with my back against the door watching you, watching the thong that is around your knee area now as you sit there. You wipe off and get up, pull your thong back up and walk over to the sink right in front of me, the large mirror in front of it magnifies our images. As you bend over to wash your hands in the sink I move towards you and wrap my hands around your waist from behind. You're surprised but you don't push me away, you straighten up and lean into me, "what are you doing?"

you whisper,

"what does it look like I'm doing?",

I whisper back, with that I start going upwards with my hands cupping your breasts. Squeezing each one hard, you turn to face me and you kiss me first, the mix of my intoxication and the lighting in this bathroom is making me dizzy or is it this mouth of yours I'm tasting for the very first time. I'm pulling the hem of your short skirt up to your waist now with my hands as you start to unbutton my shirt. I'm kissing you all over, I'm hungry for you, can you feel my desire? I raise you so you're sitting on the counter now, I want to leave your thong on, because you look so sexy in it. You're kissing my neck and sucking on it so hard I'm so going to have some explaining to do when I get home, it's obvious you want to leave your mark on me. I have your tops off already somehow, the bra too, hhhmmm I step back, let me look at you, how magnificent you are sitting there, the blackness of the area around your nipples reminds me of a ripened mulberry, they say the darker the berry the sweeter the juice and baby I want it, I need your juice, any of it, all of it... I attack them with my thirsty lips and tongue, I give them so much love and attention because I never want you to forget this very moment for as long as you live, you're loud and not quiet at all, you're screaming 'Suck me, Lick me, Do me' Please Please just FUCK me', I will, I promise I will, just let me love you first... I lick down your belly until I have to kneel before you, I spread your thighs wider apart, your thong is tight against your pussy, I start by stroking you with my fingers up and down the length of your pussy, right through the fabric of your thong. You're soaking it with your wetness with each stroke. Can you feel that, do you feel my fingers on you now?, yes I'm right there I'm touching you, say what you want to say, tell me all your dreams. All I needed was the green light to say it was ok for me to do this to you, all I needed was just one night to show you what I can do to you, just one night to change your life as you know it, yes baby after I'm done with you, you can never forget me, thank you darling for giving me this green light.. I slide your thong to one side of your pussy and I make contact with your silken flesh, your silken folds, your godly possessions. You're engorged, all the blood in you must be rushing to just this part of you at this very moment, baby can you feel my touch, how bad do you want me now, before I'm tempted to enter you with my fingers I move my mouth closer, I start from the bottom, with an out-stretched tongue I lick the length of your cunt, collecting all of the sweet and tart juices that I asked of you and you didn't disappoint, it's everywhere on my face as I lick and lick you, it's on my chin, my nose, around my lips, yes your juice is everywhere and I wouldn't have it any other way. Never has anyone been so wet under my touch, I can suck it from your clitoris, suck it out of your cunt, and when I push my tongue into your slit, it's warm and all so fucken tight, it grips at it as I forcefully fuck you with my tongue, you have your feet resting on my shoulders now, I have full access of entry into you, you're holding on to the counter, your head leaned all the way back and your body on fire... 'Eat me, eat my fucken pussy' you moan loudly, AHHhh OooHhh, Ya Ya, that's it.., I LOVEeEee it, I.. I loveeeee it.. You're moaning uncontrollably, I lick you from your ass hole all the way up and then down before I put two fingers inside of you, yes keep your legs up there for me, I want you just like that, I'm finger fucking you as I stroke your clit with my tongue, I take turns fucking you with both my tongue and my fingers, all you can do is grab on to my hair, you have my face pressed so hard against your pussy that you're making it hard for me to breathe, but I don't complain I'm loving it... I want to make a bitch out of you, but with the nasty things you're screaming you may just make a bitch out of me... You're pulling onto my hair so tight.. I know this won't be enough.. You need a complete Fucking, you want me to fuck your brains out huh? I have just the thing for you.. I say wait a minute, step back, remove my pants and panties while you touch yourself giving me that wanton look... I say I have something for you.. And I pull out the vibrating big black cork and fasten it on... I move towards you and you feel it in your hands, go under it and start to stroke my wet pussy as you kiss me once again, more passionately this time, there is no way this is your first time, you're good at it, you're kissing me as if you're in love with me, as if I'm yours, you're holding my face as you kiss me while gently pleasuring me with your fingers.. I can't take anymore Pardon my French but can I FUCK you already.. You turn around skirt still above your hips, thong still in place and heels still on and you hold on to the marble counter as you bend over looking at our reflection in the mirror we both face... Your ass is amazing from this angle, round like a black pearl that is rare to find and once again I kneel slightly and run my tongue from your hot swelling cunt to the bud of your ass hole.. it's sexy, makes me want to fuck you there but not tonight.. I stand back behind you while holding on to your waist with both hands I slide the dildo into you, I use my arms to pull you into it harder as I start to fuck you faster from behind, you're watching me in the mirror and I'm watching you, our eyes are staring deep into each others' not directly but through the mirror before us.. 'Oh baby, Fuck' you start to cry, 'I'm your fucken bitch, please fuck me harder," you cry, this makes me pump harder into you as I switch it on to vibrate, you're losing your mind and your moans become hysterical now... I'm losing control this vibrating is moving through me too.., I move my one hand to your shoulder for better grip, and now as I fuck you, you can feel every inch of this thing go deep inside of your cunt, vibrate

35

through your g-spot go past your vagina and into your cervix.., 'Are you my fucken bitch, tell me, are you my fucken slut, are you?', 'Yes, YES, I'M yours Yes just Fuck me please, Fuck meeee' I'm sweating and breathing heavy, you're sweating and breathing heavy and I just can't take my eyes off you in that mirror, this image is one many can only dream of.. I'm fucking you slow but steady, deep and hard, then faster then I slow it down all over again.. Do you feel it? I'm right there with you, I'm fucking you, do you love it, yes I'm there, I'm all there, can I make you fall in love with me just by fucking you this way?? I'm fucking you.. Tell me, tell me how good it feels... Cry baby, cry for me... This pleasure only a few ever get to experience, this dominance, this submission is utter ecstasy.. You start to convulse as I'm not relentless on you, now I have my thumb fucking your ass hole as I vibrate fuck your pussy, you can't tell me you don't like it, I'm going to make you love it, make you beg for it.... In no time I have you Cummming and Cummming.. Shit I can see your cum oozing out of you as I fuck you in and out still, not stopping.. I have silenced you, I have made you cry just from fucking you,

you had no idea what you were in for tonight... I keep the dildo deep inside of you holding you tight as my climax takes over me... My legs are shaking now, I have to hold on tight to you.. My cum is dripping out of my pussy and onto the floor.. So much of it, no one has made me cum this way.. At last I pull out, you turn to me as you hold me, tears are streaming down both our faces.. I couldn't tell you why I'm crying but I thank you for giving me the green light, for giving me this one night.

Velvet Handcuffs

I was thinking of you today when I went by the novelty store and bought us a pair of velvet handcuffs.. When I get home I want you to have the table set, serve me and feed me. You want to be a slave for me, you want to worship me.. I'm gladly willing to be your mistress. You lead me to that holy ground in the privacy of our bedroom where no secrets exist, where nothing is off limits, where you're free to explore my body and I'm free to explore yours, if you please me tonight and leave me thoroughly satisfied.. Oh the things I have in store for you my majestic slave, the ways in which I plan on rewarding you are endless. How will you please thy Goddess? How will you worship this body I give as an offering to you? You know your duty too well, you aim to please you never want to leave me wanting so you start by undressing me, then undressing yourself, you kiss me so gently, so soft, every inch of my body is blessed by your lips as I stand before you, you go behind me and kiss my back, my thighs and my ass, you come around and you kneel before me, willing to do anything I ask for, surrendering yourself to me. I part my legs and you know what that means you bring your mouth to my pussy, you lick it and make it wet, you moan with excitement at the way it tastes in your mouth, I start to trickle some honey into your mouth, you lap it up and swallow.. I love it when you drink from my body, when I quench your soul, filling every void that ever existed within you. I know I'm what you've been waiting for and now that I'm here, show me how you shall thank thee, you stroke me with your magical fingers while you suck and drink me, so tactful as if you're playing a tune on your favorite flute. Yes thy mistress is enjoying the ways you're thanking thee. The way you have your mouth open and ready to receive makes me want to bathe you with a golden shower but tonight I have a pair of Velvet handcuffs for the pleasurable torture I have in store for you. Watching you in this worship of my womanhood, gratifies me so much and soon my heavenly faucets are turned on, I moan deeply as you receive, letting my river flood your face, as you make an effort to catch every drop that comes from within me.. I'm ready for the other ways in which you satisfy me, I order you to stand, to lay your body on the bed, you obey, the first thing I do is reach for my velvet handcuffs, I bring both your arms up above your head and I chain you to the bedpost, now I've made you captive, made you my slut, made you my slave.. Does this not please you? is this not what you dream of, what your soul has been searching for, well you don't have to search no more, now that you're here, just become what you are.. A slave for me. I move to your mouth to kiss you and the taste of my pussy is still on your lips, I let my saliva

38

build then I deposit it into your mouth to help you wash my taste down,

I love it when you drink from my body, I move to your neck and I start

my assault on you kissing you, biting you with my teeth, when you walk

the streets tomorrow they will all know I made a slave out of you, don't

even think of crying already, my torture has really not begun, I move to

your nipples I bite each one so hard with my teeth, I know it feels like

they may fall off, you scream in pain but quiet down, whimpering under

your breath for you don't want me to stop, you never want me to stop.

I make them feel better by the flicking of my tongue on them by the

blowing of soft blows over them, see I can never just leave you in pain,

I lick your navel, your thighs, until I get to your feet, I grab your right

leg and I start to suck on each toe, starting with the big one, you can

only wiggle and wince, you're chained in place.. your arms won't bruise

because for you my sex slave I bought a pair of special velvet handcuffs...

with your toes in my mouth, I lick and suck, separating each one of them

with my tongue and with my free hand I reach into your center and I run

my fingers around and around, spreading the wetness from your hole to

your clit, Oh don't you love how that feels, my tongue in between your

toes, my fingers in between your lips, you're moaning and screaming

my name...' I love you my mistress' you say out loud.. You close your

eyes and arch your back, you're trying to find a way to free yourself

somehow.. But not yet baby I'm far from being done with you.. I stop

giving you a chance to catch your breath, I light a long candle and bring

it where you lay.. Helpless, bound to this bed by velvet chains... I start

to drip hot wax at the center of your chest, right between your breasts..

you cry out loudly, tears rushing out of your eyes, your body shivering in agony, I blow at the drop of wax, helping it cool and freeze against your skin, I do this all down your belly, each drop brings about the same sensation, and I give you the same comfort with each drop, your tears are streaming down the sides of your face and soaking the sheets.. But each time I ask you if I should stop you frantically nod your head no.. You love the pain of pleasure, you pleasure in pain... I blow out the candle and begin to peel off the round blobs of wax that line your torso.. I replace each blob with a wet kiss.. Loving you gently... I torture you this way only because I'm in love with you.. Can you see it when I look into your eyes? I have calmed you down, made you trust me now.. I leave you there to get a spray can of whipped cream out of the fridge.. I spray the foamy sweetness on your nipples in circles, I make a heart shape right on your belly, it's so cold.. I'm playing with your body after all its mine for the taking.. It belongs to me, you belong to me, I own you now. I pause and start to feast playfully, you moan and smile at the same time, you look so innocent so sweet as you lay there and let me feed from your body, you wish you could touch me, do something to me but your hands can't be freed, I want you to just concentrate on every sensation of the things I'm doing to you.. I love you.

When your tits and belly are clean I move in between your legs I want you to open them up, put them way up in the air for me and you do as you are told, I spray the white cream against the folds of your dark and peeking pink flesh, its dripping into you as I pour it, dripping from the top of your clitoris downwards.. all the way to the crack of your cheeks, can you feel the cold rush on your anus? Don't worry I'll make it warm again with the tip of my tongue.. when I'm satisfied with the amount of cream I have on you, how its melting against that part of you that belongs only to me I nourish myself from the center of you, with each lick I raise my head so you can watch me swallow you, your head is raised and stretched, you love to watch me eat from the center of you, if your hands were free you would have me glued to this part of you, but you're mine and I can tease you all I want, I can take my time, yes I want you to beg, beg your mistress to lick you some more.. You melt my heart when you beg me, the puppy eyes you give me make me give in to your demands, for a second I forget that I am the mistress of you and that you are my slave, so I become your slave just for a moment tell me what you want me to do to you.. Of course you want me to fuck you, so I have my middle finger inside of you while I'm still cleaning you up, I finger fuck you slowly, stopping to put my finger in my mouth and suck on the cream from inside of you, this makes you gasp.. YES YES BABY.. TAKE ME.. TAKE ME I LOVE IT I....I LOVEEE IT, FUCK ME.. OH GIVE IT TO ME I'M YOURS ... I'M ALL YOURS.. You're grinding against my face and fingers so hard you're dripping wet with sweat.. I have two fingers in you now, you're so FUCKIN WET, its easy for me to start fucking you with three now, I'm building you up slowly.. I never thought this was possible but since I have you chained to this bed and can do as I please with you, I'm going to fist you.. I'm fucking you with four fingers your moaning is getting louder, your pussy's grip on my fingers getting tighter, I struggle to keep fucking you this way, struggle to keep myself from Cumming before my task is complete.. at last your pussy is giving way I tuck my thumb between my other fingers and your cunt is only giving me partial entry, I lick around my hand helping you get wetter, with my hand working into your sweltering pit, I start to suck your clitoris into my mouth hard.. really hard, I know its intense, your heart is beating against your chest so hard, your eyes are rolling back into your head, your hips are moving up and down so violently, you're screaming and crying, I hope no one is home next door, you sound as if you're being massacred.. I guess you are... Don't pass out on me yet, I'm working to get my knuckles into you and at last your vagina gives, I start to twist my entire wrist that is now buried inside of you against your g-spot, my fist fills your every cavity, its sensation is so heightened, your muscles are clamping down on me, I can feel the blood pulsate in your inner veins, are you still with me? Even though I'm sure by now you have lost your mind, left this earth and are on a different planet now. I attempt to pump in and out and its impossible, the grip is too tight so I just twist slowly from side to side, I can clearly feel the ridges of your g-spot, its heart is beating, you let out a roar like a lioness as you seizure from your mighty orgasm, the roar is coming from deep within you, its thunderous against my ears, I CUM instantly, I don't stop, your whole body shakes and shakes, it feels as though you'll yank the chains that hold you captive as if you were a wild animal trying to gain its freedom, I can't reason with you right now.. You're on a different realm of life, you're alien to me, I've brought the beast out of you, it almost scares me.. My whole hand is drenched from the CUM coming out of you, its dripping down the entire length of my hand.. You can't stop Cumming until at last you lay still, not moving... I bet you never thought a pair of velvet handcuffs could leave you unconscious.

My Piece of Candy

We finally got ourselves out of bed around midday today, we showered together like we always do, put on our faded blue jeans and tees and drove downtown to our favorite breakfast cafe`, parking far from it just so we can stroll the brick layered sidewalks of this beautiful part of town. We walk hand in hand, people passing us by stare at us, they are not sure what to make of us, we have the same frame, our complexion couldn't be more identical, our style of dress.. yes we could so be sisters so they think, but its in the way we hold hands so intimately, the way we smile and giggle so freely that keeps them wondering, but we don't notice them, they can say what they will, think what they want, they don't know us, have no idea about the passion that exists between us, would never understand how deep our connection, how far our roots go... they have no idea that even we can't find just the words to explain this thing we have. When we get to the cafe` we order our usual eggs over easy and toast and since its such a nice day out, raspberry ice tea to top it off. As we eat my eyes are glued on only you, you would think I would finally tire from being so taken by you, how every little thing about you takes my breath away, you would think at some point hearing your voice would stop making my heart sink but it doesn't. When we finish, I pay our meal ticket, making sure I grab the piece of candy on the ticket tray.. Its the kind that you like, the soft mint that melts in your mouth.. I put it in my pocket before you notice and we take off and stroll back the same way, with the same smiles and giggles on our faces, the same intimacy in our embrace and the onlookers continue to stare but we simply don't notice, they could never understand what we have.

You've planned for us to head to the movies and its your pick this time. I already know what you will make me watch, its some romance flick, you're such a hopeless romantic, inside the theater you rest your head on my chest, I put my arm around you, we're warm and cozy as if we're in the comfort of our own home, by the time the movie is over you've shed a few tears.. 'You're such a softy' I whisper in your ear and as we leave you chase after me, wanting to get your revenge but when you catch up with me, all you do is put your arms around me, give me a light peck on the cheek and say 'A softy for you'.. You make me blush with the things you say to me, you make me feel like a little kid again, everything you do excites me. As I drive us back home, I have my free hand on your thigh, I need to have constant contact with you some how, I always have to be touching a part of you, it soothes my soul. As I get out of the car, I remember the piece of candy in my pocket, I take it out and wave it about, teasing you, telling you, you can't have it, but you surprise me by snatching it from my hands and before I know it you have it in your mouth, you rush to our door, trying as fast as you can to unlock it, but you don't make it in time, I get there, grab your hand and make you drop the keys on the floor, I have my body pushed hard against yours, so you're facing the door with no escape, I demand to have my candy back, you protest as you giggle... With your body facing the door, you twist your neck so you can get a glimpse of me behind you.. I love it when you challenge me, it makes me hot for you... right as we stand like this outside our door in broad daylight, I start to pull your t-shirt up, I don't give you room to move.. Our lips are locked now.. Your mouth tastes so good and minty, your tongue so fresh.. You let me steal the candy from you with my tongue but I suck on it just a little while, while I kiss you and deposit it back into your mouth.. You suck the new taste out of me, I have your top completely off.. I don't care if people pass by, I can't help this moment, can't help this want and need I have for you. My hands are grabbing your breasts, I still have you pinned against the door, you manage to bring your right hand behind you and into my jeans and my panties... You already know I'm wet.. As you touch me like this, I can't help but moan.... I want you so bad. I find entry into your jeans and you naughty girl you have no panties on... you make my job so easy.. We're swapping the melting minty piece of candy back and forth as we stroke each other's pussies.. I'm grinding against you with my body... I have to keep kissing you like this because if I stop I know your moans are much too loud and sure enough you would draw an audience in no time... You want to take a breath but I don't let you... with my hand around your waist and into your jeans I'm fucking you now.. Right outside our door, you have your fingers buried inside of me too.. We're doing a dance, a love dance. Lips on lips and fingers inside pussies... We've turned this hallway, way out in the open into our bedroom, I give in, release my mouth from yours and let you scream and moan away.... my own moans rise.. I love you baby and I don't care who sees. We climax at the very same time... after which we're brought back to reality and realize that we're outside the door after all.. As you gather your t-shirt on the floor our neighbor arrives, he looks our way, I look at you with a look that says, 'you should never have stolen my piece of candy', we don't say a word as we enter the door and lock it behind us...

Back Seat of My Truck

After leaving your best friend's dads' 50th birthday party we all decide to hit the club for some real music, real drinks and real dancing. Ya the party was alright but it was definitely a much older crowd and you and I had to pretend we were just friends so of course we were anxious to get out of there. It was the first time I was meeting your best friend and we seemed to click, she seems ok with the fact that you have decided to be with a woman now, all night she has been a gracious host, making sure we were enjoying the party.. She feels like really dancing too, so she drags some young boy with and joins us on our club outing.. I offer not to drink so I can drive everyone, after all it's your best friend and you two need to just have some fun tonight. You sit in the front with me while your best friend and her boy toy sit in the back.. As soon as I start driving off, I can see them in my rear view mirror making out like a pair of horny teenagers, it makes me laugh as I give you the signal to watch them, you and I giggle aloud bringing the smooching to a stop... We get to the Max our favorite gay club and it's packed, gay boys are walking around with no shirts on, flaunting their sexy bodies.. You know they got no shame, it's a shame though coz the only other lesbians we see every time we come here are the wanna be straight girls who make out with girls just so their boyfriends can watch and each time we see girls making out we get excited thinking at last another couple like us only to see the very same girl making out with some dude later on in the night. You hate it when guys try to dance with me, it gets on your nerves and I think it's so cute how you get possessive of me this way. The best is when I'm sober and you're intoxicated, watching the little drunk things you do, I buy you more and more drinks because I'm here to take care of you, your best friend and her young lad have disappeared, we're not bothered we're too into each other, we dance the night away.. From hip-hop to techno to slow jams.. We don't discriminate.. music is music.. The way you gyrate your hips in front of me, your ass massaging my crotch is super sexy, makes me want this night to be over so you can do that to me without these clothes on.. Finally 1am rolls around and it's time for the club to close already. Your friend and her friend find us at the front door and I'm so ready to drop them off so I can take you home... They're practically doing everything in my back seat except fucking.. The further intoxication at the club obviously is helping. You are giving me that look, that 'I won't be able to wait till we get home' look, without saying a word you take my free hand and put it in-between your thighs, making me massage you through the opening of your mini skirt, you've made it a habit now of not wearing any panties not even thongs.. You say they just

49

get in the way..

You're soaking, I guess a little heterosexual action got you a little hyped. I'm driving on the highway at a speed of over 70mph with my fingers between your legs and two people practically fucking in my back seat.. The windows in my truck are getting foggy, sweat running down the glass... You're really making it hard for me baby, they're moaning and groaning in the back, you're moaning and groaning in the front.... Somehow I don't get pulled over and I actually make it back to your best friend's house taking my hand away from pleasuring you, I tell them it's time for them to go, they bid farewell anxiously, I guess they will find a way to finish what they started inside. I'm not worried I just want to get you home so we can finish what you started.. As soon as we're back on the highway you take my hand again, this time you use both your arms to fuck yourself with my hand.. With both your arms holding my wrist, you pump my fingers inside of and you pull it out and do it again, I'm trying so hard to look at the road so we don't crush, you don't care.. You're driving yourself crazy, the alcohol, the speed is fueling you, I'm wet and sweating as I drive until I just can not take it any more, I pull over on the side of the highway.. It's after 2am barely any cars on the road... I start to kiss you now, start to pull your clothes apart, I rip your expensive blouse.. I don't care I just want to have you naked right here in the dead of the night on this empty highway.. You're just as crazy for me if not crazier.. The front seats are not allowing us to do what we want. Naked I jump to the back seat, naked you follow.. I couldn't explain to you how all our clothes came off so fast but they did.. I lay on my back, my knees bend, my legs open you come on top of me, but you face my

pussy and your pussy sits right above my face.. With just enough light

from the street lights of the highway I can clearly see your precious

parts right in front of my eyes, how wonderfully crafted and designed

your cunt is, your ass is perfect, you look golden.. You're already eating

my pussy as I start by running my fingers on yours as we lay in my

back seat, doing our favorite 69... Having you above me like this lets

me see every crevice on you and I love it, I hold your ass and pull your

lips into my mouth, your juices easily spill into my mouth when I lick,

suck and eat you this way. I feel intoxicated even though I know I didn't

drink.. My pussy is your playground and yours is mine for the taking,

our mouths and fingers play magic tricks on one another's moist private

parts, my tongue and fingers are in and out of your beautiful beautiful

ebony cunt, in and out of your magnificent ass hole... Until at last I just

decide to fuck you with two and then my thumb while I suck, lick and

eat you... It's so hard to concentrate when you're doing things I can't

even explain to me.. I can feel myself on the verge of explosion with the

way your crafty fingers and mouth are devouring my pussy, my ass hole..

The swallows you keep gulping as you satisfy me.. OooooHhh Oooohh

baby cum with me, Please. Please won't you cum with me... I'm begging

you please cum for me Now.. I need you to cum with me... I'm pleading

with you... Begging you please please baby please.. I want you to cum for

me so so bad... In no time you're crying out... I guess now I get to drink

too, you're intoxicating me with your natural liquor that's pouring out

of you and into my mouth that anxiously awaits it... I'm Cumming with you.. We are one and the same.. Our bodies collide... I forget where mine ends and where yours begins.. As you collapse on top of me in this very position.. We must have dozed off to sleep because when we open our eyes it's in response to a cop's knock on our foggy window..

Sunset Onto Sunrise

The remnants of the night before are scattered all over the floor of
the light peering room.. The soft leather whip, the velvet cuffs, the
candles, and clamps, the upside down lamp shade, the strap and the can
of whipped cream.. But here you lie before me, this mold of fine dust,
and sun kissed skin that is your body is heavenly. Your eyes are still
shut, I wonder what you're dreaming of... I take my arm off from
around you, remove my body from spooning you, I need to capture this
image of you in the wake of this sunrise, this golden image, this
marvelous shape... Last sunset I made you submit to all my demands and
yet here you lie now perfect like an angel with broken wings, I know I
can fix that. I know I can help you find yourself somehow, all I
needed was a chance and as I capture different frames of your image I
make a promise to myself to be the one that mends your broken wings
and makes you whole, yes I want to be the one who completes you, the
one who can finish your sentences.. Yes I understand all the different

sides of you

and I want to love them all, equally, I long to learn how to please
each.. How to heal the broken hearts, and broken trusts.. Can I be the
one? I put the camera away and I put my naked body on top of yours
while you sleep, making you think you're dreaming this but it's all
real, I'm right there with you, each time you close your eyes, do you
feel my soft kisses on your eyelids? My soft full lips against your
soft full lips, the soft, gentle and wet kisses I put all over your
face in this sunrise, the sensation of my nakedness against yours..
But still you don't open your eyes, you're caught up in your dream and
I'm caught up in this reality of you, I continue to kiss you and you
smile in your sleep, softly, gently in all the places I know you like
to be kissed, I fucked you last sunset but in the wake of this sunrise
I long to make love to you and that's exactly what I do.. You're my
sleeping angel, so peaceful and serene, I want to wake you into day in
the most delightful way, you think you're obsessed I want to show
you just how much I long to eat and taste you, love you and hold you.
When I'm all the way between your thighs you make a stir as if you'll
wake up but instead you smile again in your sleep and when I get to
the center of you, I'm surprised to find you wet and ready for my
salivating mouth, could you be playing possum? Pretending to be
asleep, do you enjoy me more this way, when you can't interfere, when
you let me decide just how to please you. When the tender flesh of my
tongue makes contact with the glowing flesh of your pussy lips,
you let out a soft moan, could you be dreaming this? I know you're

not. With all the pressure my tongue can exert I'm licking you in circles, not missing any inch of silken skin, it's wonderful when you're sleeping for you never rush me, never beg me to do anything else, I can take my time doing just what I love to do to you. In the wake of the sunset on to sunrise all I want to do is please you with my mouth, love you with my tongue and swallow the streams that flow from you. I'm not sure how long it takes, I don't keep track of the time, I could do it till sunset on to sunrise. What else could be more special than this, forget the lovers before, forget their touch you think you can't live without.. Are their words as powerful? Their hearts as open? Their spirit as free? If the answer is no then just let me love you from sunset on to sunrise.

First Time

For the first time our eyes meet at close range and nothing is said
but our faces keep coming nearer to each others'. When our lips meet
we both break and pull away because something about kissing is making
us both hyperventilate. I proceed to undo your shirt and bra and
before my eyes your perfect bosom stands at attention, rosy nipples
invitingly staring back at me. At that very moment I feel my liver
quiver, my body shiver with an instant fever. You notice I must be
going into some type of cardiac arrest and rescue me by whispering 'I
know it's your first time it's ok I'll teach you how, it's ok'. As you
softly instruct me of where and how to touch I follow the orders
eliciting a loud and excitable moan, a moan that sounds like a well
orchestrated opera in my ears. This ability I now possess to please you
in this way sends waves down my spine, a river starts to flow between my
legs, am I urinating... No a secret faucet has simply been turned on
for the first time. Never in my life would I have ever guessed this

would be possible. I'm not sure how we carried ourselves to the queen

bed of my bedroom, where you take your turn at doing the things you

just taught me to do, completing this magical act with your soft

face and the softest lips touching my other lips to which my

excitement rises to a level that threatens to render me unconscious. I

feel the biggest wave approach as I reach a climax. We both collapse

exhausted and completely out of breath. That night I made love for the

very first time to a woman whose beauty surpassed even my wildest

imagination. Of course I held you tight for the remainder of the hours

of dawn, just in case I had dreamt it all.

Public Bathroom

We're both standing there nothing is said but I never remove my gaze from yours. I move towards you and as if by a magnetic force I start to softly kiss your pretty lips, forcing you to open your mouth in response and to offer me your sweet tongue, I indulge in it for a while and then I move to your neck I leave rough wet traces as I kiss there, I place some warm breath in your ear as I whisper just how gorgeous you are. I am anxious for my mouth to meet your breasts. So I take it there circling, gently suckling on your nipples with my tongue. I massage both breasts with both hands, fingers rolling, enjoying your round erect nipples, you're moaning, you want to scream but you know we're in a public bathroom, I don't stop there. I surprise you with my strength as I lift you and place you on the sink counter, spreading your legs, lifting your little skirt above your waist, I can see your beautiful thong, I want it off, and I push your body back as I remove it with my teeth... And now looking right back at me is your glistening pussy. I want to touch those lips but I feel I want to taste it more, you're practically dripping wet, I bet you had no idea I could ever get you this excited, this horny. I bet you never thought I had the power to make you want me this bad. I now kneel before you, using my arms to keep your legs in place; my mouth and tongue meet the lips in between your thighs for the first time. I lick you up and down, circle round and round against your clit... I continue to stroke you with my powerful tongue a thousand times until you cum in my mouth, finally screaming no longer able to contain it...

For now I'll stop here for it's only our first time, sure don't want you to pass out.. If you think for a second that's impossible then think again, look baby just how much I have you so wet and bothered...

Private Dancer

A strip club was the last thing on my mind but when hanging with the boys
anything goes, so they've decided to take me to the girls girls girls show
and I protest but not much, I haven't had any eye candy in a while, we get
to the strip club kind of early and we get real good seats right in front of the
stage, the two girls dancing right now are ok but not breath taking. I order
a sex on the beach because what else does one drink in a place like this...
None of the girls on stage have grabbed my attention and watching the stout
bald gentleman who now stands next to the stage while the one girl rubs her
ass on his chest kind makes me feel nauseated, this isn't the kind of show
I want to watch, I warn my boys that if the show doesn't get better in here
then I'm finishing my drink and leaving, I've been in here just 30 minutes
but already so put off. The song ends and a new one begins, the girls exit
the stage and I happen to lift my eye from my phone and catch a glimpse of
you as you walk onto the stage with the spotlight on you... The whole place
freezes at least in my mind as if everyone in here has their eyes on you,

your dark skin is glowing under the fluorescent lighting, I can't yet clearly see the details of your body but at a distance you're shaped like a coca-cola bottle, tits perfect in your tiny lingerie blue lacy bra that matches the lacy panties that are holding your round ass in place... My mouth goes dry and I swallow trying to catch my breath, my boys are laughing now they can tell I'm almost in shock at the sight of you... You move to the center of the stage so gracefully, you grab on to the pole with both hands, somehow lift your legs up like an acrobat and you are now hanging with your legs holding you, you're so skillful, I'm tempted to get up so you notice me, so you can be my private dancer right there on that stage but I remain seated just watching, when you're done with the pole, you remove the bra and toss it right in my direction, I catch it and now your eyes are on me, you remove the lacy panties and all you have on now is just a tiny thong, I thought for a second you may toss those to me too but you don't you toss them to some dude but your eyes remain on me as you do your dance, you're clearly teasing me now... drowning me with the swaying of your hips as you move across the stage, the massaging of your tits and your belly, slowly my boys and all the people in the room begin to fade, all that's left is the light shining on you and me sitting in this chair watching... You've become my private dancer, you move towards me, I'm seated with my arms rested on the arms of the chair and my legs open in my jeans, you start to dance with your face almost touching mine and your hands holding the sides of my chair, I lick my lips, I'm getting wet but I dare not touch you I know the rules, but you must like breaking them because you start to feel my tits through my t-shirt as you dance, then you take both my hands and place them on your bare breasts making me squeeze them all while you keep dancing for me, you turn around and you start to get low shaking your round ass in front of me, ppphhhheewww I could almost pass out just from watching this.. You move your ass to my chest and I can't help myself, I grab each cheek with each of my hands and as you shake it I'm massaging your cheeks, you're so fucking sexy, you move your ass to my crotch... You're making me want to fuck you right here right now, when you turn around you surprise me by slipping your one hand down my pants, you've opened my zipper slightly but not all the way, your hand has partial entry into my jeans and you're teasing me, not quite touching my clit but just playing with the flesh above it, wow you're driving me wild. I don't know how you managed to make everything else disappear just so you can give me this private dance. When I can't take it anymore I pull you into me, make you turn and sit on me with your ass on my crotch I immediately go around your waist with my arm and bury my hand in your thong, when my fingers make contact with your pussy it's soaking wet, you're leaning into me with your head and chest as if to kiss me but you never do, you put your hand behind you and into my jeans, we start to finger fuck each other right there, we can't see anyone else, nothing exists in this moment.. We're moaning and sweating and moving our bodies against each other with such a balanced rhythm, you're a goddess of a black woman.. You feel so good that you make me want to take you home and make you my wife, I have my other hand holding you so tight against me as we fuck and fuck and fuck... I start to cum and you start to shake... I'm drowning in us, and then my alarm clock rings waking me up! Ugh I hate when that happens....

Under the Light of the Summer Moon

The night is bright not by stars but by the bright full moon of summer
that dawns it. While the children are asleep, you reach over me in our
bed and whisper 'let's go somewhere'. Quietly we slip into our fuzzy
slippers and sneak out of the door, we're trying so hard not to
giggle, I have no idea where you're taking me. You open the door to
the Jeep, I jump in and you drive us off. The sunroof is open and
through it I can see the light of the moon follow us across the dark
sky, there is a cool but comfortable breeze, as you drive, you have
your hand on my thigh. I look at you and think to myself, how so lucky
I must be to have a girlfriend as beautiful and loving as you. Even
though I have no idea where you're taking me, I'm enjoying the quiet
breezeful drive under the moonlight. The streets are dead, you turn
into the beach, park and let me out. The tides and waves of the ocean
are magnified with the silence about, the noises of the night are all
around, the crickets chirp and the sand underneath our footsteps sinks

as we walk.... The moonlight eliminates the whiteness of the sand. You

lead me with my hand in yours, you're not saying much until at last we

reach a spot where a checkered red and white cloth is laid out, two

thick rounded wine glasses lay across it, and a bottle of the South

African Ponatage lays next to them, there is something about

this very spot I instantly notice, the moon's circle surrounds it and

now as we stand there we're cast in its light while the darkness

lingers about. You start to remove my silky top then next you let my

shorts slip off me in this moonlight, I'm still trying to take it all in, the

sounds, the setting and the form that stands before me, when I help you

undress the tone of your skin glistens in this moonlight like glazed white

chocolate, you bring your lips to mine, I shiver at the taste of you, this

setting awakens every sense in me and just as the water in the ocean

crashes against the shore I feel my own river start to flow between my

legs. You're being so gentle with me tonight, you seem to be celebrating

this body that holds me, you're in worship and without you saying a word

I can tell just how much you love and adore me, with your palms you're

caressing my every curve, with your lips wetting every inch of skin on

me, when you reach my breasts, you suckle on my nipples gently, licking

up and down with your tongue, while you do this I am kissing your neck,

slightly biting, then kissing your ear, I know you love this, it makes you

moan as you suck on me as you move down my belly, you stop at my

navel and just concentrate on this area for a while then my groin, the

bone above my hips, you lay me down before you kiss me there, you take

my foot and start to lick on my toes, sucking on each one, the sensation

it gives me drives me wild that's when you start to stroke me in circles
right on my clit while you continue to suck my toes, you are going to
make me cum just by doing this and when I'm almost there that's when
you move your face to my womanhood and when your mouth reaches the
center of me that's when your worship ritual really begins, you search
every crevice with your tongue, you indulge in my scent, you drink from
my body, you thank

thee with your lips and with each stroke and soft kiss you plant down
there, I moan to the sky, as if to say yes lord I'm here and I'm open
and naked as I give this woman my soul. You don't stop making love to
me with just your mouth no matter how loud or out of breath I become,
and even as my stream continues to flow, your thirst is never quenched
for you continue to drink every single drop of me, I can no longer
count the climaxes you've taken me to the peak of the mountain top and
the deep depth of the sea so many times, I feel I may start to go
blind. I can't stop saying 'I love you', you can't stop saying you
love me, I pull you up because I need to feel your naked body on me
now, I need you to warm me, to warm my spirit. I'm holding you tight as
you fit perfectly on me, our body parts are aligned, breasts to
breasts, mounds to mounds, we start a slow grind as we kiss
passionately, softly, I feel you my darling, your wetness soaking me,
your clitoris massaging mine, even this cool breeze can't prevent the
heat that's emanating from our bodies and coating our skin, I can no
longer tell where I end and you begin, oh lord knows how much I love
your skin, we're one under the light of this summer moon. Our

souls are entwined, our bodies inseparable. Even before we climax tears are escaping us, happy tears, joyful tears... It is in that moment that I know it was wise of me to always carry that ring I have for you with me always, just waiting for the perfect moment to ask you to be my wife and for you to spend eternity with me because nothing in this world is more beautiful than this moment we have right now. Out of the blue I find myself whispering in your ear as you still lay onto of me 'Will you marry me'.... You hold me in silence and continue to worship with your lips.....

You're My Feast

Tonight I want to prepare you; I want to make a meal just out of you. As we get ready for our nightly steaming hot shower I get the jar of Vanilla Sugar Scrub in my 'bath & body works' bag, the sales lady promised me that it was sure to do wonders for you and I, she assured me that when I was all done rubbing you down with this real sugar vanilla scented scrub, your skin would be so flawless, so silky soft, so chocolaty brown, that it would glisten but most of all it would taste like sugar and vanilla...., I stand naked in our shower watching you under the hot stream of water, the water knows just how to follow the curves of your body, I watch the water trickle and fall off your nipples, your eyes are closed under the shower head, you look perfect, like an alluring angel sent down just for me to wonder at, oh how beautiful you are, how pure, how sacred. Before you open your eyes, I scoop some sugar scrub and rub it first in-between my palms and grabbing one of your arms I start to massage it, with up and down strokes my hands going in opposite directions, you start to moan slightly, I'm sure it hurts maybe just a little but I know you like how it feels against your skin. I move to your other arm and traces of sugar and oil are left coating every inch of skin that my hands have touched. When I reach your breasts, I look you right in the eyes as I massage, A small whimper escapes my lips for I am trying so hard not to get so turned on right here right now, I have your belly, thighs, legs, back and your bountiful buttocks yet to sugar scrub, so I can't get wet already baby. I close my eyes so I can't see that sexy look on your face, that look of ecstasy you have every time my hands are in worship of you. I complete my task, when I turned you around and massaged your round ass I almost passed out but I remained composed, I watch you rinse in the hot shower and ahhh does your skin radiate now, it glows so bright, you smell as if you have been dipped in the finest vanilla, it's on you, all over you. I'm anxious now to have you out of the water for the next thing I have in store for you, in our bedroom is a tube of butterscotch ice cream topping the kind that freezes in seconds, but no my darling they won't be any ice cream to pour it over, I want your body to be the dessert on which I pour this tasty treat. When you are all dry the oil from the scrub still laminates you my ravishing queen, I dry off too and lead you to our waiting bed. I start to kiss you as I lay you down, starting with your neck, baby you taste amazing, you are kissing me hungrily as well as if you can taste your scent on me. When our lips come together sparks fly, your mouth is so tantalizing, your tongue against mine is like the sweetness of a pear

so ripe, I suck on it ever so gently then I take your lips into my
mouth again, indulging in them, running my tongue across them then
across your teeth, counting each one with the tip of my tongue... Tell
me you love it baby, tell me... Instead you whisper how much you love
me... Before I'm tempted to keep moving down your body with my mouth
just this way, I grab the butterscotch topping, I straddle you with my
legs open I'm sitting across your waist, I put the tip of the tube
onto of your right nipple then I squeeze and watch the butterscotch
coat your entire nipple then trickle down the side of your breast, I
move it to your left nipple do the same thing then I bring my mouth
down and I start to blow on your butterscotch coated nipples, watching
it freeze over them like dry paint... I smile because I know that it
will take work from my tongue to have it completely licked off of
you... Are you ready my love, I'm so hungry and so thirsty, can you
feed me? Can you quench my thirst? I bring my body down on yours and I
start to feast on your nipples, with each butterscotch flavored lick,
there is still a lingering taste of vanilla from your gleaming skin,
such a blend of flavors all in one divine dish... As I lick and
swallow and lick again I reach down to your wet inviting pussy and I
start to stroke you, never removing my mouth and tongue from your
breasts... I'm feeling your excitable clit... Your fingers have found my
wanting pussy with only a few strokes of it,
you start to finger fuck me with two then three fingers... I'm so wet
so wet for you; I'm fucking you too now, all the while feasting on
your butterscotch flavored nipples... The harder you fuck me, the

69

harder I grind on you and against your invading fingers... I can feel the tightness of your pussy against my fingers, you're contracting against them, your moans are so loud and laced with tears... Cry for me baby, cry as we fuck just like this... Nothing can feel better than this baby, so cry for me. Do you see the tears that are streaming down my face and falling onto your breast...? We start to shake, to shiver; the moans are uncontrollable now... You don't have to say a word baby; I'm climaxing too right now... Orgasm so violently so gently at the same time... I'm yours; you take me every time I feast on you... When all is settled I bring my butterscotch flavored lips and quench my thirst with your flowing juices.

Fuck Me Senseless, if that's What Will Make You Feel Better

You show up unannounced, let yourself in and slam the door behind you.... I start to frantically apologize before you say a word... Before I even finish saying "baby I'm", I feel the palm of your hand slap me as hard as possible across my right cheek, "I'm sorry baby", I'm so sorry I say through streaming tears trying to walk to you, you're fuming mad, when I try to hug you, you shove me so hard with both your hands that my body slams against the wall... 'How could you, how in the world could you fuck her'? 'baby I'm so sorry' is my only response. With both your hands against my shoulders you're shaking me against the wall, I grab you by the neck with both my hands and pull your face towards mine as I forcefully kiss you, you're turning your face resisting me, pushing me away, but I'm determined to calm you down somehow, I don't want to, but maybe just to get you to stop for just one second I let go of you and slap you across the face. Giving you a taste of your own medicine... I didn't want to baby but there was just no getting your attention any other way.. You're holding on to your face and you break down in tears for the first time, 'why why why' you ask as you sob, my cries are even worse than yours, I wrap you with my arms as I start to kiss your forehead and before I get to your lips you push me against the wall once again, 'you want a good fucking? Huh? I'll show you a good fucking you hear me? I'm gonna fuck you senseless, 'baby it was you I saw when I was with her, it was all you.'.. Then how.. Before you finish you have hit me again and this time you follow it with a passionate kiss, but an angry kiss, you're pulling on my hair behind me so hard as you kiss me, then you grab at my shirt with both your hands and rip it apart, I can't believe your strength tonight.. I'm amazed and frightened all at once, you've already left my lip bleeding from your slaps.., 'Take those pants off now' you demand in a voice that's so commanding it makes me hesitate a little but I quickly unzip my pants and let them down all at once with my panties... 'Now get on all fours', I bend before you and with your clothes still on you start to rub your fingers from my clit all the way up to my ass hole.. And suddenly you thrust your fingers inside my pussy, I squeal in pain but you don't stop you're not being gentle at all, I thought maybe just maybe you would have licked me but I guess I don't deserve to be graced with your tongue tonight... With your other hand you start to fuck me in the ass with your thumb again not being gentle I want to scream in pain but I better obey and let you have your way with me, you're calling me a bitch, 'is that what you like you bitch' as you fuck me harder in both places, you keep adding and subtracting the fingers you're fucking my pussy with, as if you want to fuck me with your entire hand, you're making my pussy hurt, my ass hurt... But nothing can stop you, I'm powerless to you so I just bite hard against my bottom lip to keep from crying out... I want to beg you to stop please baby please I've had enough, I've had enough... 'I won't stop until I've fucked you senseless' I hear you say... But soon you start to tire, sweat running down you, sweat dripping from me, you finally give out and lay on the floor I lie on top of you my baby, and start to kiss your beautiful face telling you how much I love you and only you, how no one else compares to you, your touch, your lips, your body.. Mmm baby, I kiss you gently now that you're too exhausted to fight me off you, I start to undress you as I kiss every inch of skin on your body,..... Leaving traces of wet kisses making my way down to your wet and waiting pusssy.....

Mrs Ausdin, His Wife, My Woman

She is probably one of the happiest married woman you'll ever meet,
her husband is as handsome as can be, they have a perfect family, kids
just adorable, and yes he makes sure she has everthing and anything a
wife can ever need. So what is it about Mrs Ausdin that has my attention
so captivated? could it be that smile of hers with those full lips always
glossed with a dark stick, or the way her bosom sits at attention on her
chest, how could one not look, the sexy way she wears anything, the
long legs, the heels. I think secretly Mrs Ausdin loves to torture me, I
know in her mind she has it all, she is so satisfied. In my head I know
I could make her forget it all maybe just for one night, maybe just for a
brief encounter I could make Mrs Ausdin my woman.. Could I get her
wet, make her pussy throb for me, could I make her throw caution to the
wind forget her inhibitions... just for a moment, I know there is nothing
in this world she envies after, nothing more she could need, nothing
that money can buy... but I have to find a way to have her taste on the

tip of my tongue. I picture it like this, an elegant party perhaps where she shows up dressed to kill, her hubby on hand, both of them looking amazing, as always her smile is dazzling her tight black dress as short as her legs will allow, I notice her from the time they walk in, she has no idea I'm watching her every move. I may be there with someone but at this point that doesn't even matter my only focus is Mrs Ausdin, yes I see him pay close attention to her. He makes sure she always has a full glass of champagne in her hand, he looks into her eyes when they speak, she smiles at him always, they are so in love it's written all over their faces. Maybe I just can't get to this woman, maybe there is no way I can have her taste on the tip of my tongue but even if it kills me I will try to... I see her walk away from him into a back room maybe for some privacy, she is on her phone, I follow her there, we're in some kitchen no one else is about, she looks up a little surprised perhaps..'ohh I just had to get this call', 'oh you're fine' I respond meaning fine as in FINE.. and she gives me that smile, that dazzling smile... I wait till she hangs up and start some small talk about how gorgeous she looks... she giggles in response, I must be looking good too, for why else would she be melting already, as forward as it is I just ask her if she has ever kissed a woman.. ohhh now she plays shy... tries to turn and walk I block her escape and at that very moment the scent of whatever perfume she is wearing fills my nostrils.. Mmm you smell amazing I say to her.. she seems nervous I'm obviously standing too close I know.. "What are you doing to me?" she manages to say.. "what does it look like I'm doing", I say, in response, putting a hand on her leg moving it up her thigh.. my face getting closer to her neck not touching her with my lips but letting her feel my warm breath against her skin. If Mrs Ausdin really wanted to go she could have, I'm not that strong, I'm not keeping her right here in front of me by force at all. I look her in the eyes now my lips almost brushing hers but not, my mouth slightly parted but not open. Mrs Ausdin I know you've waited a long time for this, I know you've touched yourself thinking about it, I know you've soaked your panties imagining it.. I'm thinking to myself, as I stand there looking at you, your eyes are glistening as if you want to cry, maybe you just want to scream 'fuck me' already.. I don't know, I wait, you move your face closer, you part your lips, you brush them against mine just lightly, I respond by grabbing the back of your neck with both my hands and kissing you with wet kisses, I let my warm tongue invade your waiting mouth, you pull it in sucking on it, we start to breathe heavy..ohhh Mrs Ausdin what are you doing to me? you now have your arms on either side of my waist pulling my body against yours...'I want you, right here, right now you say to me'. I've waited forever to hear that.. I push you against the table and make you sit on it. I unzip your dress as I kiss your shoulders, your neck.. your breasts.. and yes that bra has to come off... We've totally forgotten where we are.... To my pleasant surprise you have no panties or tights on.. your legs are so smooth you totally could have fooled me.... I have your legs spread, I can't even believe that finally I'll have your taste on the tip of my tongue... yes you're very wet.. so wet that your wetness is trickling onto the table... I let you see my tongue as I lick your thighs making my way to your pussy... When I get there I spread your juices with the tip of my tongue.. from the bottom to the top of your clit.. your hands are grasping my hair already.. can you feel my smooth face against the skin on your thighs as I eat you? I lick your lips with a gentle force letting you feel the texture of my tongue against that part of you thats so sensitive and so sacred.. the more I lick, taste and swallow you.. the more engorged your clitoris and pussy lips get.... you're moaning and I'm moaning, as I lick you taking your lips into my mouth sucking then licking.. I'm dizzy, you're in ecstasy... how good does it feel? I bring my fingers and start to stroke your pussy lips and clit but never taking my mouth from them.... I can't wait to enter you, can't wait to introduce you to this new pleasure.. I can't wait to show you just what your body has been missing.. are you ready for me to enter you? I let two fingers into you.. finding the ridge of your g-spot, the tightness of your pussy walls against my fingers is magical.. I start to fuck you slowly...in and out all the force against your g-spot.. your clitoris in my mouth.... we're doing a steady grind on the table.. your eyes are rolling back in your head.. your head thrust back and your body is on fire, your skin is now covered in a thin film of sweat... your breath is shallow and heavy, you're gasping for air, your grip on my hair even tighter... I can hardly breathe... I'm fully dressed but my clothes are now wet from sweating my panties are soaked.. because just tasting you on the tip of my tongue made me cum... I had waited so long... Now won't you cum for me... I'm right there fucking you slowly, sucking, licking you.. I just want you to cum for me... please cum for me... can you feel my tongue on you... you're in my mouth, I'm inside of you... just cummmm for me... Yes I'm right there.. moan, scream for me..

tell me how good it feels... did you think it could ever feel this good, am I making you tremble and weak in the knees.. Yes you taste amazing, your pussy tastes so sweet.. I can't get enough of it, I can't wait to taste your cum in my mouth.. give it to me....You let out a soft but loud scream... Your pussy throbbing so much... drenching my fingers.. shaking....and you leave me with your taste on the tip of my tongue... as you hurry back to the party

Island, Books and Sex

We have been planning to get together for what seems like years now but finally it's happening, I can hardly believe it. You picked Bermuda I guess you love the fact that it is one of the few islands that has pink sandy beaches and it is only a few hours flight from the states, because of my family and schedule it had to be somewhere close and 3 days is all that I can get away for anyways. You've been so sweet about making all the arrangements, in the time we've been talking we've really gotten to know each other well, from a distance we couldn't be more opposite, I'm in the healthcare field which I once was desperately passionate about until a messy divorce derailed my plans of one day getting my PHD in Nursing, but this has only made me focus on my writing more, it is one of the things we have in common, though it's only a hobby for you. You are very content with your job as some head-honcho of some big bank. I can't even tell you how we even got to this point, we were friends really, you always referring to me as dude and I always making it a point to let you know

of all the chics I've fucked being the player I am. Then out of the

blue the seduction happened and things just haven't been the same

between us, I warned you from the start not to develop feelings for me,

and yet we both insisted on a romantic island where all we will do is,

read and make love....

I've brought some of my favorite books on my must read list. As my

plane starts to descend the view of the island is unbelievable, the

blue and green ocean, the pink sandy shores literally take my breath

away, I notice then that my palms are sweaty, could I be nervous? I'm

not sure why, but I guess it's the thought of finally seeing you face

to face. You arrived before I did so you could get the car rental and

all that taken care of by the time I got there.... I packed lightly

just a carry on bag, I have my torn tight jeans, a tight t-shirt and

high tops on... I also wear my shades as I walk out to look for you, a

deliberate move to avoid your eyes when I first see you... I don't

take too many steps before I see your face in the crowd of those

waiting, you have such a radiant smile, my hands are in my pocket, I

look down and walk towards you but I can't hide the grin on my face.

You embrace me, putting your arms around me, I hug you so tightly like

a long lost friend. Holding you this way gives me a warmth I didn't

expect. You lead me to where the rental car is parked as we engage in

small talk about my flight. When we step out into the sun, the warm

air coats our skin, it smells nothing like the cold midwest air of

Nebraska that I'm used to. In the parking lot you grab my hand as we walk, it makes me freeze, there is something about you that is already giving me all kinds of sensations. As soon as I'm sitting on the passenger side I remove my shades and for the first time our eyes meet, we just look at each other for what seems like an eternity before you say to me, 'I have been wanting to kiss these lips for so long', but what you don't know is that I have been salivating from the minute I saw your radiant smile, I move closer and brush my lips against yours so lightly as you close your eyes, you return the kiss with your warm tongue invading my mouth, I'm immediately wet, I close my eyes and let the wetness and texture of your tongue in my mouth intoxicate me, ohh baby can you feel the gentleness of my sucking? we are kissing so slowly, so passionately, we take turns exchanging warm wet tongues, swapping saliva, I have to break it off before I start to take your clothes off right here.. I pull away. You start to drive to our hotel, the building is beautiful but at this very moment I really don't notice all the beauty that surrounds us, no words are spoken as we walk to our room that has a huge glass door that overlooks the ocean, the curtains to it are wide open letting the glow of sun shine right through... I have to shower since I've been sitting on a plane... I'm in there 5 minutes tops and when I walk out with a white towel wrapped around my body you have Janet jackson's 'that's the way love goes' playing in the room... The words filter through my mind, 'like a moth to a flame burned by the fire, my love is blind can't you see my desire'. Over and over after all that's why we

81

are here I do want to make you crazy, I want to give you the time of

your life, take you places you've never been before... You're in the

kitchen pouring us some wine and I come and wrap my arms around you

from behind, kissing the back of your neck, I just want to go deeper

and deeper as Janet sings but I'm taking it slowly. My hands are under

your shirt now, caressing, feeling you, I start to make my way up to

your breasts but I change my mind and start heading in the opposite

direction to unzip your shorts.. I do and my fingers find their way

into your panties as my mouth bites and sucks at your neck, you're

holding on to the counter almost in a trance, I can feel you just

taking it all in, I know you truly want to taste every kiss and touch

of mine right inside of you, your only response is the shallow rapid

breathing and moans, my towel has fallen off, my naked body is glued

to you, my pussy right against your ass, my fingers now tracing the

shaping of your clitoris, my other hand pulling your shorts and

panties down, I purposefully take too long playing with your clit

because I want to make sure that when I move them further down to your

opening you're completely dripping wet for me, you can't take it any

longer, so with your hand you force mine further down, my fingers slide

and two of them enter you, with you at the controls, you start to slow

fuck yourself with my fingers, bearing down with each stroke forcing

them to penetrate you deep each time, I'm losing it, I fuck you with

three then four then back to two again, I'm grinding against your ass

so much that I want to fuck you from behind, I plant kisses down your

back as I withdraw my fingers out of you, you're protesting 'no baby,

please don't stop fucking me please', I'm not stopping I just want to
fuck you better. You instinctively bend over using the countertop as
your anchor. I kneel behind you so that when I look up your pussy is
open right at my mouth, in all its honey wetness I devour it, slapping
up the slippery juices, sucking, licking, swallowing, fucking you with
my tongue, removing my mouth only to bite and kiss at your things, I
bring my right hand up and working my fingers in and out of you with
the help of my mouth and tongue, you are just so wet that four fingers
inside of you feel like two so I put all my fingers of my right hand
inside of you. You gasp as if you're in pain and let out a yell but
then you force yourself down swallowing my entire fist, I'm inside of
you up to my wrist, it feels so tight that I'm afraid I may be hurting
you, your juices are coating my hand and dripping all the way down my
elbow then to the floor.. Each time I pump myself deep within your
walls, I can feel you tighten and squeeze my fist, I can feel your
thoughts, I can feel the pleasure I'm giving you, you want to say
something each time but you can't speak, you can only scream and moan,
I can feel myself start to shake with orgasm, I can feel your legs
start to tremble as you start to cum, your pussy walls are pulsating
against my hand inside of you, you're flooding me and piercing my ears
with the sounds of your climax, it seems as if we have been fucking
for hours and even when I stop and gently work my way out of your
pussy I can tell you are not yet done with me, in a daze you take my
hand and lead me to the bedroom, I get a glance of the ocean view

outside the window, the books you have stacked on a table, but it's your sexual arousal that fills up this whole place. I shut my mind off to everything else, I could stay here forever in this moment with you, my thoughts become foggy as you take me, on this exotic island.

Dancing Naked in the Rain

It has been a long exhausting day of lecture after lecture. Instead of heading to the library to study like I usually do, I decide to stop at a downtown cafe, have myself a hot cup of coffee while I look over my notes. I'm still in my white scrubs from clinical rotations early that morning. It's a cool summer evening, even though it was warm all day. It's starting to sprinkle a little, the kind of sprinkles that cause a little steam to rise off the pavement lifting the heat soaked by the earlier sun rays. I walk into my favorite cafe downtown and find myself a comfortable booth in a corner. I spread my books on the table before I even order my first cup of coffee. When the waiter comes to take my order, I say 'black, decaf, no sweetener' without lifting my eyes from my notes, but at that very instant I hear a soft but rather loud giggle coming from a center table of the cafe. I'm forced to look up in the direction of the sweet noise and that's when I first notice you, you look familiar, those big eyes I'm certain I've seen before. I'm transfixed on you, you're stirring your piping hot beverage with a spoon. You have long slender fingers with perfectly manicured nails, you are woman in every sense of the word, voluptuous in the sense that from what I can see everything is rounded on you. "will that be all?" the waitress shakes me from my daydream. 'Uhm yes that will be all' I say back to her. When she walks away the handsome gentleman you're sitting across from becomes visible to me, the instigator of your sweet giggles, I feel a tinge of jealousy on a complete stranger. You seem enthroned in deep conversation with him now, but I suddenly remember where I've seen your face, those big dreamy eyes of yours, I've seen them before. I've passed you in the hallways of my college campus a time or two. In my head I'm trying to figure out if you're a student like I am or maybe a faculty member at the school. You dress to the nines, heels, short tight skirts, I may have seen you with glasses on too, but tonight you don't have them on, which might explain why I can't get over your gorgeous eyes. I was so focused on studying when I walked in here but now all I want to do is find a way to start a conversation with you. You must have heard my silent wishes and God must be answering my silent prayers because you look up and you catch me with my eyes glued on you, you smile so serene as if to say I can see you are there.

I try to take sips of my coffee which has gotten cold, your companion must have somewhere to be, before long he gets up and gives you a peck on the cheek and exits the cafe. My mind is now spinning in circles, I know I have to find some courage to get off my seat and talk to you. I keep throwing glances towards you, I'm fidgeting with my pen like a high school kid with a crush on his teacher. I finally just will myself up, "excuse me, do you go to Creighton by any chance?", 'oh I... I'm actually a Chemistry instructor there', you respond nervously. You seem to recognize me too now, your face softens as you extend a hand out towards me in greeting. All at once our soon to begin conversation is drowned out by the rain that is now pouring heavily outside, almost obscuring all visibility to the outside through the frosted glass walls of the cafe. 'Well you better sit down, it looks like we are stuck here', you say to me... "stuck? I have an umbrella, I don't know about you", I tease, it makes you giggle, flashing your white, evenly cut and evenly spread jewels that are your teeth. I run back to my table and gather my books quickly into my backpack, in such a hurry in case you change your mind. I laugh at how silly I'm being, soon I'm sitting opposite of you with my half empty cup in my hand, luckily the waiter comes by to refresh both our cups. I talk about my Pharmacology major but the scent of you, your perfume is so intoxicating I can hardly concentrate. You seem to have a hard time looking right at me because you keep looking down, you're clearly shy even though at this point I have no idea why you would be.

About 30 minutes go by with no signs of the pouring rain ceasing, you say you have to go, I offer to walk you to your car since I have an umbrella. We signal for our tickets from the waiter, each leave cash on the table and get up to leave. You tell me you're parked in the back alley, since parking downtown is sometimes hard to come by. As soon as we are out the door it is obvious to me that the umbrella I have will do nothing to shield one of us let alone the both of us... I shout for you to lead the way, pulling you in closer to shield you from the rain. As we start to walk fast and laugh at the same time... I'm so ecstatic right now that I'm not even thinking about the books I have in my backpack that could totally get ruined in the rain. We can't walk too fast you have heels on, we are walking briskly just getting soaked by the pouring rain, I'm trying hard to cover you as much as possible, you seem to be worried about your purse getting wet, you have it clutched underneath your armpit. We get to your car and the streets are completely abandoned there is not a single person in sight, its a little dark out now but the street lights make you so visible right in front of me as you fidget with your key and I try to shield you from the rain. When you open your car door you throw your purse in the car but you close the door and stand with your back on the car and facing me. My jaw hits the floor, my heart starts racing, you're soaking wet, your white shirt is now see through, your white bra exposed against your dark skin, your nipples frozen hard by the cold droplets. Time freezes, I feel myself dropping everything I'm holding, first the umbrella then the backpack, I feel my clothes clinging to my skin as if I've just dived in a pool of water. I wipe the rain from my face, you don't remove your gaze from me, I move closer to kiss you, press my body against yours... I'm surprised at how hungrily you're kissing me as the water hits relentlessly against our bodies. I start to unbutton the buttons on your shirt, slip it off your shoulders and do the same with your bra, you have goosebumps all over. I'm at your neck kissing, sucking the raindrops from your skin until I have your nipples in my mouth, its moans and the sound of water against the car top, I'm lost shaking from both cold and ecstasy.... Your fingers are entangled in my dredlocks, I'm back up biting your bottom lip, my hands both moving down to your waist, forcing the tight wet skirt off you with whatever else you have on underneath of it.. they all drop down to your ankles and now I have you naked, my hands and mouth dancing against your body in the rain.. for what seems like forever my fingers feel some warmth, its hot in between your legs and ohhh this wet, richer thicker wetness seems to be washing the rain away from my fingers now... we are dancing in the rain, fucking, making love as if in a dream. We move to the hood of the car, you sit on it, you pull me in, you want my clothes off, I guess it would be lonely to be the only one naked at a time as this...I let you unclothe me, I'm shivering in the cold, I need to feel the warmth of your skin against mine, I need, I want, I'm yearning, begging.... BLEEP BLEEP BLEEP... I'm awakened by my alarm clock.

Will there Ever be Closure

I'm standing at your door, my heart pounding almost right out of my chest, my mind racing at a million miles per second, my palms sweaty, then you open the door and everything that was happening to my body is intensified by infinity as if my body is going into fight or flight mode and yet I remain calm while I look at you.. Why in the world would you do this to me? I haven't seen you in months, the lines between our friendship were becoming clouded after we first kissed. You had ravaged my body with just a quick short hesitant kiss, on this very door step I find myself standing now. you literally made my soul climax with just a kiss. Then for whatever reason you told yourself you couldn't be around me. You had a man and I had a woman, no secret there but it just didn't matter anytime we were in the same room in was as if we had been thrown into some magnetic field, our bodies electric charged, unable to control the force moving them towards each other... You couldn't take it, it was simply too overwhelming for you. You are straight and the question becomes why do I make you feel this way? All these years I've known you, I've never imagined this. So when you told me you just could no longer be friends I respected your wishes and kept my distance no matter how painful missing you became.

Today out of the blue I received a text from you that read 'I am not scared of you' I was annoyed at first, frustrated at the way you make my heart and emotions your personal yo-yo, bringing me close when you feel like and pushing me away when you feel overwhelmed. Never the less you sounded sweet and apologetic in your texts and I jumped at the opportunity to come over, catch up and watch a movie with you and now here you are with eyes the color of the sky, your hair shorter and complimenting your radiant face, your smile taking my breath away... that short dress hugging your lovely curves while leaving your sexy legs exposed to my wondering eyes. You give me that hug that you always give me, holding me tight and close, taking me in, placing smiles simultaneously in my heart and on my face... When I step into your living room I stop right in my tracks, your living room walls are a different color from the last time I was here... in the three or so months that I haven't seen you, you have done a complete makeover of your house as well as yourself. The only light that illuminates the room is that of flickering candles you have lit in every corner. My first thought is 'movie huh?' If there is a job you do well my darling it is that of confusing me, I'm completely perplexed. I only hear from you after months of silence and when I show up this is what you have waiting for me? HONESTLY? What kind of torturous game is this? You seem at ease, I'm trying to read you but each time I try to look directly into your eyes you look away like you have always done long before we ever admitted our attraction. What is it you hide behind those deep magical pools of green? maybe tonight I will get to find out. You say your TV is in your bedroom and we make our way there. You leading the way and I not minding at all because I like to look at you when you don't notice where on your body my eyes are focused.

You place the movie in the DVD player and I'm awkwardly standing by your bed, not knowing whether to sit down or lay down on it to watch the movie, but lucky for me you soon invite me to lay next to you on the bed while the movie plays... You have fewer candles in here, creating a cozy atmosphere. I make myself comfortable even though what's going on in my body and how I appear are completely in direct opposition. I want to feel your body on mine and yet I put my arms above my head as if relaxed. I notice you fidget with your fingers which leads me to finally look right at you and ask 'do I make you nervous?', you respond by asking me the same question, I then respond by moving closer to you but before I'm face to face with you, you have grabbed my face with both your hands, kissing me hungrily, kissing me as if you have been waiting for this kiss all your life... I'm on top of you running my tongue down the length of your neck but you say 'wait' and push me off, you get up and turn the TV off, I guess you want some music on instead... which is a relief because for a second there I was thinking you were back to being overwhelmed and pushing me away again..... I suggest J Holiday radio on Pandora and search for it on my Htc phone.. J Holiday immediately starts to serenade us with his smooth voice and romantic lyrics... but instead of 'putting you to bed' like he insists as he sings.. I'm standing next to it, undressing you while planting kisses on every inch of newly exposed skin. The contrast of my dark glowing skin against your perfect ivory skin tone is intoxicating.. You are undressing me too, I guess I have imagined this and fantasized about it for so long but now that I'm actually experiencing it, it is so surreal, an intense irrational reality of a dream.

Your lips are so soft each time you place them on me it feels like I'm being hit by wet fluffy cotton. We make our way back to the bed doing a dance between ecstasy and romance, fingertips, nipples and lips trading touch as we move... I don't know what you had planned for this evening with me but now my plan is to make you pay for all those nights you kept my mind awake struggling to figure out what the heck we are to one another, all the times you teased me with your kisses only to push me away because it was too much for you. I lay you down and straddle you in my nakedness and with both hands I cup each of your breasts, kneading them like bread dough, I'm kissing your mouth running my tongue along the outline of your pearly white teeth then the shape of your plump lips, lightly biting at your chin before placing intermittent love bites of gentle sucking of the skin on both sides of your neck... You are moaning now slowly.. almost in exasperation..... I have no idea what you are thinking and at this point I really don't care for I am far from being done with you. I'm making my way down on you, patiently so you will never forget. If you thought you were overwhelmed before then after tonight you may just lose your mind.

When I finally have one of your nipples in my mouth, you dig both your hands into my dreads, pulling tightly on the ropes that make my hair.... as your OOOOOOOOOOS & ahhhhhhhhhs get louder.... Your body is my playground right now, I'm taking full advantage of this moment.. I flip you over onto your stomach.. and trace kisses from your shoulder blade all the way down to the mountains that make your round ass, massaging you there, stroking your entire back as if giving you a sponge bath with my tongue..... I'm getting impatient for a taste of what has been steaming in-between your legs this entire time, so I flip you back over and sweep over your belly and navel but when I get to your pubic bone.. I stop, raise my head and watch you with your body on fire and your head thrown back... I'm lost in this moment but you bring me back by commanding me to 'come here', pulling me back to your face by my neck.. 'I just want to kiss you baby, please just let me kiss you'... I need you stop making my heart melt by calling me baby... when I'm finally looking down on you from above, you take my lower lip into your mouth, half sucking and half biting... it feels soooooo good I can't breathe, you are sucking the life out of me... I need some oxygen to save my life I must go back where I wanted to be.. my face between your thighs... before I do so I start to gently rub your clit with the fingers of my entire left hand... you're steaming hot alright, supple like wet velvet... with this new contact you exhale as if you had been underwater and are just now coming up for some air... with that reaction and in one sweeping motion I move down your body, raising both your legs up from behind your knees... releasing the suction of your mouth from mine only to plug the suction of my mouth to your clearly engorged clitoris.. by the time two of my fingers enter you, you are no longer here... I can no longer recognise the person you have become... who are you? While I have you like this I want you to experience every side of me... so I let you catch your breath as I lay on the bed, but within seconds I'm telling you to 'Come here'.. sit on my face.. let me show you what your body has been missing.....

You grab a hold of the metal posts of your bed and lower yourself down onto me... and I'm back again doing my magic tricks on you... with the red slender dragon that lives in-between my lips... breathing fire and throwing hot molten lava into you.. my fingers sipping magic all over inside and outside of your skin..... All of a sudden you cut yourself from all the invisible chains that have been binding you... you scream for me to 'eat your pussy'... your voice strong and determined... you are fucking the shit out of me now, the way you are riding my face I can feel you breaking blood vessels in the veins that line my lips.. I will be walking around with some messed up lips tomorrow.... you are covering my hand with the fingers inside of you down to my elbow with your excitable juices... Your skin is covered in sweat, my skin is covered in sweat.. our bodies are now a wet mess of moisture.. some pouring out of our pores, most coming from within our bodies... you are completely drunk and high off my love, you try unsuccessfully to remove yourself from the grip of my mouth and hands.. as you shower me with evidence of your climax... and even though I have never used any drugs, I abruptly become addicted to the drug that is you.... In this moment I now know all your secrets... we are 'insieme'.. Italian word for 'together'... you have become the yin to my yang.... and in my orgasmic haze I finally let you go.. and you lie exhausted next to me.. no words are exchanged but we start to kiss.... starting all over the interchange of the unspoken emotions and deep affection that exists between you and I.... each time clothes are put back on, clothes end up completely off again...... until our bodies are sore... that was months ago.. I wonder will there ever be closure?

My Instant Addiction

It eats me up inside that I can't have you, that I have to wait indefinitely for that which I want most. You whimpering, trying to call out my name but only soft moans escape your mouth, your body frail and exhausted from the many times we've made love & have made each other cum.... But It's all in my head, I know the rules I'm not allowed to be alone in the same room with you. So I take what I can have for now, the times you can get away to see me, the walks, keeping a distance from you even though I never really want to let go of your hand.... So in the few moments I can wrap my arms around you on this public city sidewalk, heaven descends to greet me, as if everything I've been through my entire life has led me to just that moment so I can truly appreciate it, wallow it in, float a little, experience perfect peace.

This body of yours that has your life story written all over it, is magnificent through my eyes even though pages that tell the story of you and I are yet to be written on it. Walking with someone has never felt so serene, amidst the splattering rain showers your warmth gives me comfort. While I'm lost in you all of a sudden you embrace me, just like you did on the night you became my instant addiction, that embrace that molds me into you... Fitting perfectly like the missing piece to the puzzle. It makes me dizzy when our faces touch, my nose against yours, looking at your smooth skin at such close range, trying my best not to place love bites across your neck, force you to taste the sweetness on my tongue, finally get the taste of your saliva in my mouth. Have I ever told you just how sexy you are? That you have me walking around swollen in a constant state of arousal, that I want nothing more than to take your hand and bury it in my pants so your fingers can get saturated by what you do to me.... While we stand in this intimate embrace on this public sidewalk I start to imagine we are behind my door in my apartment, the place you're so afraid of. I imagine that finally our lips can touch without breaking and even though we are both shaking, our trembling hands are finding pieces of bare skin to caress on the other's body. Right behind that door I lift your teasing t-shirt off, take your bra off, my fingertips and the palms of both my hands making contact with your nipples then cupping your full breasts, my mouth unable to detach from yours. You shouldn't have made me wait so long baby. I want to take it slow, lick and taste every part of you, but most importantly I want to know what making you cum sounds like, feels like and tastes like. I want you to give that to me.. my gift from you. A gift from your soul... I'm too impatient to take your jeans off, all I need is the zip and button undone so my fingers can find their way inside of you... What I want is to be face to face with every part of you, your nipples, your belly, the inside of your thighs... Suck on your fingers one at a time... Can you feel your pussy getting wetter when I do that... Will your clit just invite me to take it into my mouth. Will your wetness beg me to lick it without stopping, will tasting you for the very first time just take my breath away... Will you be able to breathe baby when my warm tongue is coming in and out of you, will you pull on my hair and push me in as far as I can go... Will you make me taste you deep? Will you make me work hard for your tears of ecstasy, will you need my fingers rubbing against your g-spot gently while my mouth sucks on your engorged clitoris to reach an orgasmic climax... What will it take baby? I just want to show you how beautiful these hands of mine can really be. Don't think for one second you're addicted to me yet, let me make love to you first and you'll soon have a new meaning to 'Instant addiction'!

About the Author

Ruth Marimo was born and raised in the Southern African country of Zimbabwe. She has lived in the United States since the year 1999 and has chronicled her immigration struggles as well as her coming out process in her memoir titled: 'Outsider - Crossing Borders, Breaking Rules, Gaining Pride'. Writing is a work of passion for Ruth. She owns a small residential and commercial cleaning business to support her two children who are the center of her world. She is an Activist and Speaker who is passionate about echoing the voices of the marginalized, from undocumented immigrants to sexual minorities throughout the world. You can learn more about Ruth by visiting her website: www. ruthmarimo.com, connect with her on social media @Ruth Marimo Author, @marimoruth twitter.